Charles L. Youngblood

# Adventures of Chas. L. Youngblood

during ten Years on the Plains

Charles L. Youngblood

**Adventures of Chas. L. Youngblood**
*during ten Years on the Plains*

ISBN/EAN: 9783741123740

Manufactured in Europe, USA, Canada, Australia, Japa

Cover: Foto ©Andreas Hilbeck / pixelio.de

Manufactured and distributed by brebook publishing software
(www.brebook.com)

Charles L. Youngblood

**Adventures of Chas. L. Youngblood**

# ADVENTURES

OF

# CHAS. L. YOUNGBLOOD

DURING

# TEN YEARS ON THE PLAINS.

COMPILED FROM HIS OWN JOURNAL.

BOONVILLE, IND:

BOONVILLE STANDARD CO., PRINTERS.

1882.

# PREFACE.

In presenting this little volume to the public
I have no apology to offer nor any explanation
to make to the inception of the work, except
that it was written at the request of many of
my friends, who, knowing of my life in the
West, were anxious to have my adventures
written and published according to the fashion
of the day.

Concerning the work itself I have only this
to say: It is not fanciful description of imaginary adventures, but a true recital of a few of
my hunts on the plains and such other occurrences as might be considered worthy of
mention. These are not altogether in the
order of their occurrence but as I call them to
mind, and in most instances dates are omitted
on account of incompleteness in my data.

And now I leave it with you, necessarily
incomplete and imperfect as it is, and even if
it does not come up to your expectations from

a romantic point of view, I can assure you that I have kept within the bounds of truth, which I hope will make up for all it may lack as to romance.                    C. L. Y.

## DEDICATION.

To my aged father whose paternal care and affection has been so constantly manifested toward me during my whole life this little volume is affectionately dedicated by the author.

# CONTENTS.

# ADVENTURES

OF

# CHARLES L. YOUNGBLOOD

DURING

## TEN YEARS ON THE PLAINS

———————:✳:———————

## CHAPTER I.

### INTRODUCTION.

THE author of this sketch was born in Anderson township, Warrick county, Indiana, April 9th, 1826. His father was a native of South Carolina, and his mother hailed from Virginia. The first forty years of his life was spent in the place of his nativity, during which time he was engaged in farming. His education was just rudimentary, only such as could be obtained in the primitive log school house with its big open fire-place. The old-fashioned schoolmaster armed with rod and ferule, the roaring log fire and the blue-backed spell-

(2)

ing-book are among the many things of childhood to which memory often reverts, and the mind of the writer loves to look back upon those early times when the log-rollings, the quiltings, the wood-choppings, the camp-meetings, and the thousand and one different occasions of gatherings together of the people. It does seem to me that people were less selfish and careless of their neighbors' welfare: they certainly were more kind and friendly then than now. But times and things have changed; the days of the husking-bee, the camp-meeting and the old-fashioned spelling-school have passed away, and everybody is now on a grand rush to get rich or great.

Perhaps it was because of the decay of primitive customs, and the change in surroundings, coupled with a kind of veneration for things of ye olden times, that caused the writer to grow tired of the new order of things and turn his longing eyes to the West for a repitition of the things of his boyhood.

Finally, in 1865, this yearning for the joys of the rough and tumble life of the backwoods became so strong, that, bidding adieu to relations and friends, he took his wife and children and turning his face westward, and traveling across Illinois and Missouri, brought up in Kansas City, which was then but a small town on the line between Missouri and Kansas.

At this point his life and adventures in the West, which it is the purpose of the following pages to relate, begin, and this little introduction is closed, hoping that the mind of the reader is prepared to follow him through his narrative, with at least an ordinary degree of interest.

## CHAPTER II.

SPECULATION — POULTRY RAISING — A MAN
KILLED BY A BEAR, ETC.

WHEN I arrived at Kansas City, in 1865, it
was such a little, unpromising looking place
that I conceived a dislike for it immediately.
I had money enough to have bought it almost
entire, and, in the light of recent developments, have regretted a thousand times that
I did not do so. The squalid village of a few
huts, has, in the sixteen intervening years,
grown to be a thriving, busy city of several
thousand inhabitants. Its situation upon one
of the main lines of travel and emigration,
makes it certain to become one of the princi-
pal western cities, but the prejudice I first
conceived against the place was so strong that
I failed to discover any future for it, and prevented my making any speculation on the
place.

I remained here but a short time, and then
pushed forward up into Kansas, but did not
like the country. It was so totally different

to what I had been accustomed, that I could not make up my mind to locate there. I had been used to ten-acre fields, and the broad unfenced prairie did not suit me. I was raised in a country where there was plenty of timber, and did not see how I could get along without it. So despairing of suiting myself in such a country, I turned back to Missouri. Here I finally bought a large farm near the center of the State, where I remained until 1872.

While living here I suffered considerably from what is commonly called "bad luck," but perhaps a better name for most instances of this class would be mismanagement. But be this as it may, I managed to sink several thousand dollars in real estate. A railroad route had been surveyed through the section, and a town laid out. As work was already begun on the proposed railroad, I thought it would be safe to invest on the strength of it. I accordingly purchased a good part of the town at a big price. The railroad fell through, and my town lots depreciated until I was compelled to almost give them away. I missed it in not buying Kansas City, and also missed it in buying an imaginary city.

Disheartened at my loss I determined to "go west" again, and accordingly started out with about two hundred bushels of dried fruit and a lot of butter. I did not try Kansas this time, but went to Denver, Colorado. From Denver I went to Golden City, thence to Black Hawk City, Central City and Nevada City.

Here I sold my produce and began to cast my eyes about to see what I should do. Every thing and everybody seemed to be in a hurry; even the mountains seemed to move, out of pure sympathy with every thing about them.

Every man I could see seemed on a rush for money, and that he was getting it. Men do not all dig gold and silver here to make money. I noticed many engaged in occupations that no man in Warrick county would at all think of engaging in. Among the other queer avocations that are followed out here, I noticed a poultry ranche. It seemed to me, at first sight, that this was about as nearly nothing as any business I ever heard of, but I found upon in-

quiry that it was not so small after all. The
ranche was about five miles from the mines,
where thousands of miners were at work, and
in the neighborhood were several boarding
houses, some of which had as many as fifteen
hundred boarders, and the poultry man found
ready sale at high prices for the products of
his ranche. Besides this there were a great
deal of scraps, crumbs and the like about these
boarding houses that he got merely for taking
it out of the way, which made good food for
the poultry. This made the expense of the
ranche small, and he received from fifty
cents to one dollar a piece for chickens, and
about the same per dozen for eggs, of which
he was selling at that time about ninety dozen
a day. He had about two thousand hens besides other poultry, and as the labor was light,
the expense small and the prices enormous, he
was making money rapidly in the poultry
business.

In this part of the country I received about
my first impressions of the animals of the
West. I happened one day to be passing a

house, where a man, who had just had a fight
with a cinnamon bear, had been placed. Of
course on hearing this I dropped in and heard
the fatally wounded man, as far as he was
able, relate the circumstances. He had shot
and badly wounded the bear, and was following its trail, hoping to be able to kill it, through
a rough stony place, and as he was going along
as noiselessly as he could for the rocks, he suddenly came upon it and did not have time to
shoot before it sprang upon him and dashed
him to the ground. In his struggles to release
himself from the animal, both his legs were
broken, and he saw that his only chance was
in strategy, as he was match for the bear in
strength, and he lay perfectly still as if dead,
when the bear after eyeing him closely for a
moment or two started slowly away. As soon
as the bear was a few feet off he raised on his
hands and knees—his legs both being broken
below the knee—and started to crawl away.
This attracted the bear's attention and it
turned and pounced upon him with greater
fury than before, this time breaking one of his

wrists. He resorted to the same stratagem as before, but waited until the brute was out of sight, when he again started to crawl toward home, dragging himself through the snow which was about four inches deep. A few moments after the struggle, his brother happened to be passing that way and seeing the the marks of the fight, not knowing that it was his brother who had been torn nearly to pieces, went on the trail of the bear, which, when overtaken, was for another fight, but a repeating rifle proved too much for it, and he soon had it safely dead. He then started back to see who the man was who had been in the clutches of the bear, and his feelings may be better imagined than described, when, after following it about half a mile, he found it was his brother. The wounded man had crawled that distance with one wrist and both legs broken. The poor fellow was in great agony and lived but a few hours. His father said he would have the bear skinned and sleep on the hide as long as he lived.

A few days after this I fell in with some old
(3)

hunters at Golden City, who were just on the eve of starting out on a big buffalo hunt, and I thought that here was a chance to have some sport, and perhaps make some money. Some of my readers are perhaps not aware that sport is not by any means the whole object in buffalo hunting, but many men have almost made fortunes in the business. The flesh is excellent and when properly cured is readily sold at good figures, and the hides are no drag on the hunter's hands.

While we were cleaning up our guns preparatory to starting out on the hunt, I came very near getting into a little difficulty. I thoughtlessly put a charge in my gun and fired it out of the door at random. Almost immediately a policeman came running across the street, and taking hold of my arm said,

"Come along, sir."

I saw that I was in an awkward predicament, and concluded, like a great many men who are caught in uglier scrapes, to try the insanity dodge, which I played so successfully that he said he would let me off this time, but warned me against repeating the offense. It is useless to add that I was very careful after this not to fire any more random shots in town.

After making all necessary preparations we started out to get some buffaloes, and in the next chapter my readers will find a full account of my first buffalo hunt.

# CHAPTER III.

OUT FOR A HUNT — A MISSING OVERCOAT —
MY FIRST BUFFALO — INDIANS ON, THE
TRAMP — "OLD POISON SLINGER," ETC.

THREE other men and myself left Golden
City to go about eighty miles in search of
buffalo. The first game we struck was a herd
of antelope, into which we fired, killing one.
We then went to a house about a mile off to
stay over night. We proposed to the man of
the house to furnish the meat and he furnish
the rest. He replied by saying that he would
do so. Of course we thought it was all right,
and our antelope went free, but the next
morning he charged us five dollars for his
hospitality. This seemed very mean, but the
boys contrived a way to get even with
him. He had been telling of a new overcoat,
for which he paid fourteen dollars the day before, and when we left the coat went too. He
had his five dollars, and we had his fourteen

dollar overcoat.    As it was a partnership coat we took turn about in wearing it.

We travelled on until we came to what ought to have been "good hunting," but as we saw no buffalo we were at quite a loss to know how to get them, as there was no timber in which we could conceal ourselves, it being an open prairie with not a tree for many miles. While preparations for camping were being made, I went about twenty miles from the railroad and struck a herd of buffalo.   I was careful not to get too close to them for two reasons: a herd of those animals, to a novice, look simply frightful; and I was afraid they would take fright and run away.   When I was within about five hundred yards of them I aimed at the herd and fired, and had the supreme satisfaction of seeing my first buffalo fall.   I was too much elated to try to get any more just then, though I might easily have done so, but went back to camp to relate what I had done, and we were soon on our way after my buffalo.   While on the way we saw a large one coming nearly toward us on the run. I left the others and got right in the animal's course and lay down to conceal myself, and as soon as he was near enough I fired and saw the wool fly off him, but he kept on coming. I put in another cartridge and fired again, when he dashed right at me, and I began to think that I had gotten into a rather bad scrape, but when within a few steps of me, to my infinite relief he fell dead. I afterward found out that I had not done anything wonderful, but I thought at the time that I knew all about killing buffalo. We resumed our journey, and had gone but a short distance when I noticed a large herd about a mile off. I started and went as close as I thought safe and killed one, and immediately the others rallied round it bellowing and tossing their heads. I thought this a good chance, so I kept blazing away until I got eight. I was certain then that I was the champion buffalo killer of the plains. We soon dressed them and started back to camp. We had gone but a short distance when we saw a large band of Indians coming toward us, which caused us not a little anxiety until we discovered that they were friends. There were about fifteen hundred of them and they had a permit from the Government to hunt for thirty days. This was the first large band of Indians I had seen, and it was quite a sight to me. The warriors were in front, followed by the squaws and luggage. The papooses, or babies, were lashed on horses, which were turned loose and driven in a kind of herd. Besides the papooses, the luggage was lashed on the pack horses and were driven by the squaws, while the men rode on before at their ease. The weather was very cold and it was snowing at the time, and pelting the little papooses in the face and on the hands, but they seemed to be tough enough and were taking it easy, laughing and crowing and their little black eyes shining like black beads.

Buffalo meat was low and it did not pay much to save it, and we went hunting just for the hides, and in a few days had killed over a hundred, which we skinned and left the carcasses to rot on the prairie.

As we were going into camp one day I saw three buffalo lying down, and, having only five cartridges, slipped up as close as I could get and killed two and wounded the other. One cartridge failed to fire, and I went back to the wagon to take the cap off, but while I was picking it out it exploded, nearly tearing my hand off. This laid me up for nearly two weeks.

One day while my hand was sore and I could not use my gun, I was strolling along a branch, I heard an unusnal noise, and looking up saw the "tips" of some Indians, I could not tell how many, just as they passed over a ridge. As soon as I saw them I lay flat down, and they passed on without seeing me, and it was well for me that they did not, for they were hostile and, as I did not have my gun, would have made short work of me. I met them often after that, but was generally better prepared for them, as I always had my "old poison slinger" with me.

"Old poison slinger" is the name that the men gave my gun. It was a Sharp's rifle, 50 calibre, made to load and shoot eight times a minute. It would throw a ball to kill a distance of five miles. I have killed buffalo with it at a mile, and have shot with it so far that I had plenty of time to take my head from it and see the ball strike.

Soon after I hurt my hand two of the men went off, and there were only myself and another man left, but he was a good shot and we got along very well. We were out shooting one day back about 20 miles on Cold Hell Creek, and, besides killing several buffalo, we wounded one cow that lay down and my partner went out to kill her. Before he got very close to her, she sprang to her feet and made a dash at him. The reader will bear in mind that a buffalo, when badly wounded, gets desperate, and will rush headlong at its enemy with a force that makes it very much safer to be out of the way. When he saw what she meant he dropped on one knee, and taking rest on the other, waited until she was within twelve feet of him, when he fired, hitting her in the jaw, stunning her, and

(4)

before she had time to recover shot her through the heart.

A few days after this we went about twenty miles east of Cold Hell Creek, on the bed of the Republican river, where we remained and hunted about two weeks. We were here two or three days before we saw any buffalo, but on getting up one morning and going out a mile or two, we saw the largest herd that I ever saw anywhere. I could not tell how far east and west they extended. They came in a run that shook the ground like an earthquake, and frightened our horses and made them almost unmanageable. They were all that day and night in passing. We wondered what could be the cause for such a large herd passing on a run, but found out that the Cheyenne Indians and the Utes had been fighting, and the Utes, being driven back, fired the prairie to prevent pursuit. This fire in the big tall grass of the prairie drove the buffalo, antelope and wolves out. We kept firing on them and killed one hundred and three while they were passing. We could have killed as many more, but stopped occasionally to skin what we had killed. We were compelled to remain up all night on account of our horses, and besides we could not have slept for the noise. The heavy, continual thunder of their tramp, and their incessant bellowing, made so much noise that sleep was out of the question, even though circumstances were otherwise favorable. I have seen a great many herds of buffalo but never before, or since, have seen one equal to this.

## CHAPTER IV.

BAD INDIANS—BUFFALO CHIPS—A FRIGHT-
ENED HUNTER—NOT QUITE DEAD YET, ETC.

IT was not long before the Indians became
so bad that hunters were compelled to go in
squads of from eight to ten and upwards, and
then it was with more or less risk. Hunters
were killed almost every day, but the Indians
are generally to cowardly to make an attack
with anything like equal numbers. Their
favorite plan is for a large band to surround
about three or four whites, and shoot them
down or put them to death by torture. I
will not stop here to describe any of their
methods of torture, but will do so in another
chapter.

I remember one time that I was one of a
squad of ten buffalo hunters when a band of
Ogallahs came over from their reservation on
a thirty days' permit from Uncle Sam to hunt
not far from us, and one day a squad of them
came over to our camp and got to horse-racing

with some of our boys. They were running "one horse for the other," and the Indians lost their horses. They then put up their guns and lost them. They did not seem to be much chagrined over their loss, but shook hands with us all around and were entirely too friendly, so much so as to arouse our suspicions and render us very uneasy. As soon as they left we brought our horses up close, got our supper as soon as we could, put out our camp-fire, put our guns in fighting trim, and prepared for the attack that we felt sure would come.

About two hours after dark we discovered them coming. Their object evidently was to get their horses back and steal some of ours, and, if they caught us off our guard, kill us. We waited until they were as close as we thought they ought to come, and then opened fire on them with our repeating rifles. This was wholly unexpected to them, as they had depended on taking us by surprise, and all that could run did so. Some of our men sprang on their horses and pursued them a short distance, and helped them to hurry along to their camp.

We did not sleep much that night, and did not leave camp at all the next day, knowing that we wonld have some kind of settlement to make with them, and about 10 o'clock in the morning we noticed a large squad of them coming toward us. The reader must not forget that the Indian is Uncle Sam's pet, and we did not dare do anything unless we were attacked, but had gotten everything in readiness by the time they came up. The chief, who spoke fair English, said: "You d—d —— —— —— killed four of my men out there," pointing to where four dead Ogallahs lay.

One of our men, Hank Miller, said "Pawnees," meaning that it was the Pawnees that had killed them, but the old chief roared out "Pawnees, no Pawnees," and drawing his finger around his head to indicate that had it been the Pawnees that killed his men, they would have scalped them, which, of course, we did not do, expressed his utter disbelief by saying "Poo, poo, poo, no Pawnee."

They sat on their horses and bandied words

with us for some time, watching very closely for apportunity to make a dash on us, but we were in readiness for them. We had our guns in our hands, with our thumbs on the hammer and our fingers on the trigger. We could have shot in a second, and dropped ten Indians, and they knew it. Seeing that it would not be at all easy to punish us, they soon rode away muttering imprecations on us as they went. They did not disturb us any more, and we resumed our hunting as usual for thirty days, averaging a hundred buffalo a day.

At the close of this hunt I went back to Missouri, and remained about six months. when I again started west. I made arrangements with A. Buckmaster and L. J. Shilder at Warrensburg, Mo., to sell meat for me, and took two men, Louis Allred and Silas McFerrin, with me. After about fourteen days travel we came to "good hunting." Buffaloes were plentiful and I made an average of eight a day. The hides and flesh of eight good buffalo are worth about $50, so you see it was paying me pretty well.

We were camped on what is called Sappy river, and were twenty miles from timber. While here the snow fell about twelve inches deep, and we were compelled to remain in our tent three days without fuel, the snow storm coming so suddenly as to prevent our laying in a supply. We only had a small amount gathered, and it consisted mostly of buffalo chips, which is simply the sun-dried excrement of the buffalo. It will probably seem to many of my readers in the East, that it would make very poor fuel, but in this section of the country it is preferred over wood or coal for many purposes. I have seen hotter fires made from it than I ever saw from wood. Some of my readers might have a little delicacy about using such fuel, but here it is nothing to see ladies gathering it in their aprons. In nearly every house you can find a sack full of it standing in the corner, and when the fire gets low, the lady of the house takes a few chips from the sack and puts them in the stove, and nothing more is thought of it than when you put a stick of wood on the fire, or a lump of coal on the grate. We managed to get along without getting frozen, and after the snow went off we resumed our hunting.

The two men who were with me were no hunters, and I had them employed to help me take care of the buffaloes after they were killed. One day when we were out I had killed several very close together, and while we were skinning them, we saw, about a mile away, a big buffalo coming nearly toward us, and Louis Allred said to me, "Charlie, let me shoot that one." "All right," I replied, "there is the gun." "I just want to kill one," said he, "to be able to say that I killed a buffalo." I handed him the gun and the cartridge belt, and he stalked off like an old soldier. The buffalo was lost and was running as hard as it could, looking for company, right toward him. By the time he was two hundred yards from us, the buffalo was pretty close to him and still coming, and looking pretty scary. He brought down the gun as if he were going to shoot, but as the buffalo kept coming he concluded to get out of the way, and started

(5)

back toward us for dear life. As soon as the buffalo saw him it turned and ran too, but he supposed it was right after him and was expecting at every step to be caught, and made his tracks as fast and as far apart as he could, while the buffalo was going as fast as it could in an opposite direction. He looked a little sheepish when he brought up and saw the buffalo away off and running as fast as he could in another direction, but he thought he had run a frightful risk and was not at all anxious after that to have it said that he "killed a buffalo."

Another time he and I were out together and were skinning several buffalo that we had killed. We came to one that was not quite dead, so I said that I would whet my knife while it was dying. I laid down my gun, and had hardly commenced sharpening my knife, when Allred screamed "Look out! Look out!" I raised my head and saw that it was nearly on us. I had not time to pick up my gun and had to run without it. The animal stopped at the gun and began pawing it, and horning my coat, which, in my haste, I had left lying by the gun.   As I had but the one gun, we could only stand and wait, but in a few moments it lay down right by the gun, and in about two hours died.

## CHAPTER V.

WE MOVE TO SMOKY RIVER — THE INDIANS
GO THROUGH OUR CAMP.

WE finally moved from Sappy river to
what is called Smoky river. This is only a
small stream, not being over a rod or so wide.
Along the banks are a few willows, and occasionally a cottonwood tree rises up into the
air. As this was a good place to stay awhile
we set to work killing buffalo, drying the fore
quarters and selling the hind quarters. From
this place I sent a large quantity to Buckmaster and Shidler, my agents, in Missouri.

While here I took Allred and started to go
to a herd of buffalo that I had, with the aid
of my field glass, discovered about three
miles off, leaving McFerrin to load cartridges.
A short time after we left, a band of Indians,
who had doubtless been watching our camp,
came in sight. McFerrin dodged out of the
camp and ran into the bluffs on the river bank
and hid himself in the bushes where he could

watch them. They approached cautiously, and, after firing several shots into the tent, dashed up and took possession. After rifling my camp of whatever they wanted, they moved off about a quarter of a mile and hid under a hill side, on the road leading from Wallace to the Republican river—a road much frequented by hunters—and watched the road until a man named Charles Brown, who was driving a team and wagon, came along. Brown, who was one of a squad of hunters, was driving to Smoky river to build a fire and prepare for camping; the others were a mile or two behind skinning some buffaloes that they had killed. When he was near enough the red skins fired on him, and he jumped off the wagon and started to run, but was soon struck by a ball and fell, when one of the Indians ran up to him and shot him through the head. They then began going through the wagon, but before they had secured their plunder the rest of Brown's party came up, and the red devils made themselves scarce. As soon as the hunters saw the Indians they took the horses out of the harness and pursued, but failed to overtake them.

While all this was transpiring I was about three miles away, killing and skinning buffalo, in blissful ignorance of everything else. I had just finished skinning and started after one I had wounded. The ground was uneven and as I was nearly at the top of a knoll I caught a glimpse of something just going over a hill, and remarked to Allred "There is a herd, now," and ran to the top of the hill to shoot. It was getting late in the evening and fast getting dark, and when I reached the top of the hill I could see several objects coming in sight about two hundred yards to my right, which I soon discovered to be mounted men, but could not tell whether they were red skins or white men. As soon as they saw me they dismounted and began to make signs to me, but which I did not care about answering. I did not know just what to do, and came near firing on them, but concluded to await developments. At last one of them mounted his horse and came toward us, when

Allred said "It is an Indian; shoot him." I put my gun to my face and he called to us, and we knew then that he was a white man. When he was a little closer he said "Don't shoot, Youngblood; I came very near shooting you. We were just after some Indians and they passed over that ridge as you came in sight. I am glad, now, that I didn't shoot. They killed one of our boys up at the road about three miles from here, and we want you to go up there and put him on the wagon so the wolves won't get him." We promised him we would do so, and started toward camp. We had gone but a short distance when we found an empty powder can, which, on examination, proved to be mine. I knew by this that the red devils had gone through my camp, and had perhaps killed McFerrin and stolen everything I had.

It was quite dark before we arrived at camp, and when we got within a short distance began to approach very cautiously, as we thought that perhaps they had left a detachment to take care of us when we came back.

We pushed on to where they had killed Brown, but, as it was too dark to find anything but the wagon, we concluded to go to camp and return when the moon rose, and put the body away. When we were within about two hundred yards of camp, I told Allred to wait, while I went ahead and made a kind of reconnoissance. As I was slipping along I spied the bulk of an object standing on a little rise. I thought it was a person, and, as I was standing very still and watching it very closely, I heard a very low voice saying: "Is that you, Charlie?" I then knew that it was McFerrin, and answered that it was me. He then came to me and said: "There are Indians here; they stole everything you had that they wanted. They took your horses, and shot at me, and I ran and hid in the bluffs where they could not find me." He said he was nearly frozen, and told me that he had seen them kill a man just out on the road. The moon soon came up, and we went down to the road and found the poor fellow. He was frozen stiff, and I put him on my shoulder and carried and laid him on the wagon, so that the wolves could not get to him.

We then went back to camp, when I found that the Indians had cleaned me out entirely. We remained in camp that night, and did not dare to make much light as we were afraid the red skins were still hovering about us. In the morning I saw a squad of men about a half a mile from camp and went to them. They knew nothing of the raid, and I told them all about it, then we went down to the wagon where Brown lay dead and frozen stiff. The sight of him raised their ire, and vengeance was sworn against the red skins. In a short time Brown's companions, who had been chasing the Indians during the night, returned, but without being able to come up with them.

We all held a council of war, and it was unanimously agreed to follow, and, if possible, punish the Indians. We made up a company of twenty-six men and started after them. We were all armed with long range repeating

(6)

rifles, and were supplied with from 100 to 600
cartridges each. We followed the trail for
about seventy-five miles, but without finding
the foe. The trail led us through some very
dangerous places, several times through deep
gorges and ravines, where we might have
been ambushed and every one of us killed,
with perfect safety to the enemy. But we did
not stop to think of danger, and pressed steadily
on until checked by a severe snow storm.
The snow fell about eight inches deep, and as
we had been depending entirely upon the
grass for feed for our horses, this was a serious
impediment to our progress. We could get
along well enough ourselves by killing buffalo
and antelope for food, but we could not pro-
vide for our horses. We agreed in council to
go to Fort Wallace and get provender for our
horses, and then continue the chase. We in-
formed the commander of the fort of our
business, and requested him to furnish us with
sufficient feed for our horses during the
pursuit, but, instead of doing so, he sent a
dispatch to General Pope at Leavenworth

acquainting him with the facts, and received
in reply orders to send fifty men and four
scouts to chastise the marauders. The four
scouts were Hank Campbell, Louis Allred,
Bill Peach and myself.

We took up the trail where we had left it,
and had followed it some miles, when one of
the soldiers said, "Yonder is a herd of buffalo."
The captain examined the herd through his
field glass a moment and then said, "There
they are, boys; if you want meat, here is a
chance for it. They are Indians, and well
armed." He ordered a halt, rolled out several
boxes of cartridges and told us to take all we
could carry. The Indians, meanwhile, were
collecting, and making preparations for an
attack. We were ordered to get into line.
The teams were left under guard, and we
moved on the enemy. The ground was level
for two miles, and we went at a gallop until
within a half a mile of them, when the chief
raised a flag of truce and came toward us
followed by four of his men. We stopped,
and when they were within a few hundred

yards, the captain sent two of our men out to
parley with them. They met about a hundred yards in front of us, but no sooner had
they done so than the red skins immediately
surrounded our men. Suspecting treachery,
we made a dash and surrounded the five
Indians.

The parley was not at all satisfactory, as
the Indians persisted in not understanding us.
While the parley was in progress one of the
Indians carelessly rode off a few steps and
entered a ravine. He rode into this until we
could only see him from the eyes up, and he
sat there watching our every movement.

Failing to get anything at all satisfactory
from the chief during the parley, the captain
ordered them disarmed. Eight of us covered
them with our guns while they were disarmed.
As soon as we seized them, the one in the
ravine dashed away down the ravine, keeping
himself out of danger as long as he could,
then he dashed over a hill into the band of
Indians.

The Indians greatly outnumbered us and

were as well armed as we were, and had the advantage in position. Our commander did not think it prudent to attack them where they were, but endeavored by various artifices to get them to change their position, but they stood their ground. The captain would not allow us to fire upon them where they were, as they had with them two German girls, whom they had taken alive the day before, after murdering the rest of the family, and, at that distance, we were as apt to kill them as Indians. After considerable maneuvering the captain decided to return with his four prisoners to Fort Wallace, and report the situation to the post commander. Accordingly the four Indians were placed under a strong guard behind the wagons, and we set out for the fort. The power of endurance manifested by these Indians during the journey to Fort Wallace surprised me. The weather was intensely cold, and a raw, bitter blast swept over the prairie almost freezing us to death. We had overcoats, overshoes and mittens, and yet our feet, fingers, ears and noses were frostbitten. The Indians did not seem to suffer at all from the cold, although they were nearly naked. Besides, we could get off and walk occasionally to stir our blood, but they were compelled to ride all the way. The post doctor said that they were all right, and not at all injured by the cold, though they had only moccasins on their feet and but little clothing on their bodies.

On the way to the fort, one of our prisoners made a dash to get away but was shot down; the others were turned over to Colonel Han-bright, and what became of them after that I never learned.

I did not remain with the troops long enough to know whether they made any further attempt to punish the Indians or recapture the German girls, but found a man named Riley, who had a good team, which we hitched to my wagon, and started out on another hunt.

# CHAPTER VI.

GOOD LUCK—MORE INDIANS—SOME OF THEM
DIE SUDDENLY—WHITE WOMEN'S SCALPS—
HOW THE INDIANS HUNT BUFFALO—THE
JOYS OF AN INDIAN SQUAW, ETC.

RILEY and I hunted about four weeks, during which time we killed and dried about one hundred buffalo. The game soon left and moved about one hundred miles east, near the heads of several streams, viz.: Salim, Sappy, Soloman, Prairie Dog, Beaver and Big Timber. We followed them and secured great numbers. Here we fell in with three other men, which increased our number to five. We were hunting together, and one day left one man at the camp to smoke meat while the rest of us took the team and went out for buffalo. As he was out gathering fuel on that particular morning, he heard a racket in the camp, and, supposing that we were driving in, stepped back to see what we were coming in so early for. Instead is seeing us he saw fourteen redskins going through the camp. They had taken his gun, and as soon as they saw him, fired on him. He took to his heels and ran along a ravine, followed closely by several of the Indians. We were not far from camp, and as soon as the red skins saw us they stopped and beat a retreat. They did not go back to the camp, however, but joined the rest of the band in a cane-brake on Sappy Creek, where, the next day, thirty-seven of them died very suddenly. Two white men also died about the same time. One of the Indians that was killed was a chief. He had a roll tied on his side, which one of the men took off, saying, "What is this" and when he had unrolled it, "What is it, sure enough?" We looked and saw that it was a dressed buckskin cape, ornamented with white women's scalps. Yet there are those who say "The poor Indian," and bestow upon them any amount of misplaced pity, by my acquaintance with them does not develop any traits in their character or disposition worthy

respect. Of course they are mistreated sometimes, but this does not make them any better.
By nature they are lazy, cruel, vindictive, and
a perfect type of treachery, never acting in
good faith except they can gain a point by so
doing. Mercy is a virtue which an Indian
knows nothing about, and the truth never falls
from his lips if a lie can be made to answer.
They are in all respects, as nearly as I can
describe them, veritable demons, who spare
neither age nor sex, who respect no law, and
whose chief delight is to murder, burn and
ravage.

The little occurrence mentioned above oc-
curred in April, '76, and I hunted there until
the fall without any further molestation from
the red devils. They remembered our long
range repeating rifles for a long time afterward.

While here a large band of Ute Indians
came into our neighborhood on a permit to
hunt thirty days, and for the benefit of my
readers, I will now describe, as well as I can,
their manner of hunting and killing buffalo.
(7)

They first select their place for a camp. generally near some stream convenient to fuel and water. As soon as the place is chosen the squaws set to work unpacking the goods and chattels and putting up the tents—the squaws do all the drudgery—and making things comfortable. Besides the work mentioned above they must care for the horses, get fuel and water, in fact do all the drudgery, while the men roll on the grass in the shade and smoke their pipes at their ease. When the camp is all in order one Indian is sent out to find a herd of buffalo, and as soon as he discovers one he returns to camp and reports. Then the women get the horses, and the men and boys mount their ponies and ride for the herd. The women follow, driving the pack-horses, and taking their knives to dress the game that the men kill.

A band of Indians mounted and equipped for a buffalo chase presents a very unique appearance. Their ponies are scrawny looking little things, and many are so small, and the rider so large, that his feet nearly reaches the ground. Notwithstanding his size and appearance, there is no discount on the pony; he makes up in grit and endurance what he lacks in size, and will carry a rider or a heavy pack farther in a day than an ordinary horse. The Indian's saddle is a mechanical curiosity. It is made with two forked sticks, one behind and one before, held apart by two pieces of board, one on either side, and have straps of buckskin running lengthwise. The boards which hold the forked sticks apart are on the bottom, and rest on the horse's back, while the buckskin straps are on top, and form a soft seat for the rider. Though this saddle is easy on the rider, it is frequently severe on the pony, the boards frequently being left naked, and I have seen ponies so lacerated by them that the back-bone in places was left perfectly bare. But an Indian has no mercy for his horse any more than he has for his squaw, and so long as he can ride along easily he cares not whether his pony is suffering, and will even beat him for flinching and "giving down" under one of these barbarous saddles. They depend a great deal on ceremonies for "good luck" in killing game, and the performance of these rites is almost as much of a sight, to a person not accustomed to their ways, as a good circus. As soon as they get as close to a herd as they dare, they dismount and begin their ceremonies, which consist of an immense amount of foolishness. The white man, when he starts for a herd goes right up and commences killing, but the Indian must stop and go through the rites that have been handed down to him from time immemorial. They get down on their knees and repeat several ceremonies. They talk to the buffalo and tell them not to run away as they will give them some tobacco, of which each Indian buries a small piece in the ground; they pull their horses' tails, whisper in their ears, and tie eagle feathers in their tails to make them swift. Frequently they kill a dog and eat it. All this, and a great deal more that I have not time or space to mention, is done that good luck may attend their chase. The ceremonies concluded, they mount their ponies and ride rapidly to the herd, which, if not disturbed by the powow, is quietly grazing on the prairie. As soon as the buffalo discover their foe they take the alarm, and very frequently rush in a mass directly toward them, but, when within a short distance, they suddenly whirl and dash bellowing in the opposite direction.

The turning of the buffaloes is the signal for the attack, and then the Indians, with the wildest of yells imaginable, dash upon them with their guns, spears, bows and arrows and commence the slaughter. Those with guns ride to one side of the fleeing herd, and, keeping parallel to them, load and fire as fast as they can, bringing down a buffalo at almost every shot; while those with spears, and other weapons of a like sort, rush into the herd and riding almost against one thrust the weapon almost through it in the most vital part. The Indians with bows and arrows ride into the herd as do the spearmen, and leaving the pony to take his way, use both hands shooting arrows into first one and then another. Their

arrows are often tipped with pieces of saw-
blade, on the edges of which is cut a fine
beard, which causes them to work inward as
the animal runs. They shoot three or four
arrows into one buffalo, and then single out
another, and, the arrows working in, they soon
fail and die. This slaughter is kept up until
quite frequently every one of the herd is killed.
In the hunt which I saw, they killed a hundred
and ten in less than fifteen minutes.

As soon as the killing is over the squaws
dress the meat and pack it on the horses,
while the men and boys take a rest and
a smoke, and laugh and talk of the exploits of each other during the chase.
When the game is dressed the men mount
their horses and ride joyfully toward camp,
while the squaws follow driving the pack
horses laden with the flesh and hides.

Though the Indians use the bearded tips on
their arrows in hunting, they use an entirely
entirely different one in fighting. They have
some way by which they poison them, so that
they cause almost certain death, or, at least, a

very ugly sore. Just how they poison them
I am not able to say from actual knowledge,
but persons who have been much among them
tell me that to do it they take a piece of fresh
meat, and, making a rattlesnake angry, let it
bite the meat and inject its venom into it.
The meat is then left to putrefy, by which
time it is thoroughly permeated with the
poison, and the arrows are then poisoned by
sticking them into the poisoned meat. These
poisoned arrows are carefully kept separate
from those to be used in hunting.

They frequently fight among themselves,
and more of them are killed in this way
than by white men. They exhibit terrible
ferocity and unrelenting cruelty in their wars
with each other, and those they take prisoners are always put to the torture.

A friend of mine named Van Meter related
to me the particulars of a torture which he
witnessed while among the Ogallah-Sioux
Indians.

A band of Ogallahs had been out one
day and had a little skirmish with a squad of

the Crows, and came in with one prisoner. He was a warrior about twenty, and arrangements were soon made to put him to the torture. He was stripped and tied firmly to a wagon wheel. Next, a large pine plank was shaved into splinters. Then one was selected to apply the torture, and the rest prepared to execute the war-dance around him. The one selected to torture him took a knife, and taking up a piece of his flesh between his fingers plunged the knife through it, then thrust into the wound a bunch of the pine splinters, which were then set on fire and allowed to burn out. As soon as one bunch of splinters died out, another was inserted in a fresh gash as before. The process was kept up until the skin was crisped all over the body. Notwithstanding the agony he must have suffered, he never murmured nor gave any other signs of pain, but appeared more unconcerned than most people would to simply witness such torture. During the whole time the torture was going on the Indians danced around their victim in the most wierd and unearthly manner, motioning as if they would strike him with their tomahawks or spears, and uttering the most fiendish yells and cries. When his skin was burnt to a crisp all over him, and he was nearly dead, he was toma- hawked and scalped. This, though horrible, is of frequent occurrence among the Indians. In this respect they are even more cruel toward each other than toward the whites.

## CHAPTER VII.

A CHANGE—A NIGHT WITH THE WOLVES—
BLACK-TAILED DEER—FEROCIOUS ANIMALS
—BACK TO THE PLAINS.

NOT long after the occurrences mentioned in the preceeding chapter I moved about a hundred miles south, on what is called Silver Lake. I was compelled to leave on account of the Indians chasing all the buffalo out. They chase them on horseback, and drive them sometimes as far as two hundred miles.

Silver Lake is situated near the head of Pawnee River, between this stream and "White Woman" Creek, in a large cane-brake. The reader may perhaps smile at some of the queer names applied to streams and such other natural objects. A great many were named by the Indians, who always name them from some occurrence of the locality, or from some other similar suggestion.

"White Woman" Creek derives its name from a rather sad occurrence, which I will relate. A widow named Harn was several years ago taken captive by the Indians and carried away prisoner. On their journey they camped for the night on the bank of this creek, and before they left the next morning they drove a large stake through her body and left her; hence the name. By some it is called "Suffering Woman." I notice that in a published account of a fight, which Colonel Lewis had with the Indians on this creek, three years ago, in which fight Lewis and five of his men were killed, it is called "Spanish Woman," but all frontiersmen call it "White Woman."

Between "White Woman" Creek and Pawnee River is a large tract of very low, flat country, covered in many places by large lakes and dense cane-brakes. The one on which I camped was the Silver Lake, before mentioned. When I came to this place, brought no one with me, and consequently was all alone in the midst of a broad lonely swamp, my only company being buffalo and antelope by day and wolves by night, and the latter, especially, were more familiar than agreeable.

I remember that one day I went out and kille a buffalo, and moved my wagon near it. As it was late in the evening, and the way to camp hard to find, I determined to stay out all night. So I made my bed on the ground, and spread the skin of the buffalo over me with the wooly side down. I had hardly fallen asleep, when the wolves, attracted by the smell of the buffalo, began gathering from the thickets. They soon devoured the buffalo, and began to venture near enough to pull and tug at the hide, which I was using for a quilt, and try to take it away from me. My gun was in the wagon, and I did not dare to get up to get it for fear they might make a meal of me. I managed to keep them frightened away until finally they left. The wolves in this section subsist chiefly on the carcasses of buffalo left by hunters, who kill them for their hides, and as no hunters had been in the locality for some-time the wolves were very hungry, and would sometimes even attack men or horses.

I remained in this place about a month, and had fair success in killing buffalo, but had very little market for the meat. I soon fell in with a man by the name of Fred Armstrong, who said he was a "regular world beater" at killing buffalo and deer. He urged me to go into the mountains with him to kill black-tailed deer. He told me he had just come from there, and that the mountains were covered with them. It was about two hundred miles, but I finally consented, and one morning, bright and early, we started. Our road lay through a strip of country where game was very scarce, and, as we started with only a small supply which we soon exhausted, we got very hungry. Finally, one day Armstrong said he was going to shoot a calf, since cattle were so plentiful and game so scarce, and took up his gun to shoot a yearling that happened to be separated from the herd. Just then three cow-boys rode up. This made Armstrong look a little wild. He said, "Lord, God; I'm glad I didn't shoot. for they would have been on us before the calf could get done kicking." But the cow-boys never knew his intentions, and it was well for him that they did not. As it was they rode along with us to a spring, near which they said there was plenty of deer.

We camped for the night by the spring, and in the morning I took my gun and went out to see if I could get some of them. Before I had gone a quarter of a mile, I saw plenty of tracks and began to keep a lookout for the deer. I walked cautiously up a hill, and when near the the top peered over and had the satisfaction of seeing four walking single file along a cow path. I aimed at the leader, which was a fine doe, and at the crack of the gun she sunk to the ground. Two more shots brought down two more deer. The fourth was a large buck and came running up to the bluff to near where I stood, but I was ready for him too, and wound up his career in a twinkling. I then went in and got a horse, and, putting three of the deer on him, led him along toward camp. On the way I met Armstroug, who looked a little surprised, and said, "Hello! If that is the way you are going to do, I will have to take back what I said about being a 'world beater.'" We hunted together about two months, and as I averaged killing about six deer to his one I ceased to look upon him as a "world beater." After we had hunted there a few weeks a man came to our camp to see us. One day during his visit he was in conversation with Armstrong and asked him what kind of a hunter I was. Armstrong said I was a poor shot, but the luckiest killer he ever saw. Shortly afterward he came to me and asked me "what for a hunter" Armstrong was. I told him that Armstrong was a very good hunter but was just about the poorest killer I ever was acquainted with. He broke out in a hearty laugh, and then told me what Armstrong had said about me.

We had not been there long when we discovered that there were animals in the locality other than deer, especially mountain lions and panthers. These animals will generally be found in almost all places frequented by deer, on which they chiefly subsist. They climb a tree which has a limb extending over a path used by the deer, or conceal themselves behind something near the path, and as the deer pass along under or near them, they spring upon it and kill it. They are particula·ly fond of the blood, and commonly tear the throat of their victim and drink it as it flows warm from the veins. They also eat the flesh and can carry off a full-grown deer. I was killing deer one day and wounded one, but as I was following it I discovered a large drove of them, and concluded to let the wounded one go and get some of the drove, intending to come back and get it later. I did not get to come back until the next morning, and, taking up the trail where I had left it off the day before, followed it but a short distance, when I came to where the ground gave unmistakable evidences of a struggle. After an examination I was convinced that the the wounded deer had been attacked and carried off by some animal or other. Anxious to know more of it I followed the trail, which was not at all hard to trace, as the hair of the deer had been rubbed off on the stones and the fresh stains of blood were easy to see. I had followed the trail about a half a mile when I found the entrails of the deer lying on the ground. The entrails were not torn to pieces, but, on the the contrary, were entire, and looked as though some skillful hunter had taken them out with a knife. This greatly surprised me and I began to look cautiously around to see if I could discover what it was, when, within about twenty paces of where I stood, a mountain lion suddenly raised up from the ground and, before I had time to shoot, darted into a thick clump of bushes. However I managed to fire just as it disappeared, but must have missed it. I was afraid to follow it into the thicket, and ran up on a cliff near by to shoot it as it passed out on the other side. But in this I was disappointed as it did not show itself. I waited for some time hoping to be able to get a fair shot at it, but its stomach was well filled off the deer, and I suppose it lay down in the thicket and went to sleep for the day, at any rate, I never saw it again. The panthers were even more numerous and more dangerous than the mountain lions, and when we had fresh

(9)

meat in the camp they would yell all around us the whole night. Their yells make a person unused to it not a little uneasy, but one soon gets accustomed to it, and in a few nights pays no more attention to it, than the people in Indiana do to the hooting of the night owl.

I remained here hunting until the snow began to melt in the mountains, when the deer left me. The black-tailed deer lives in the mountains, except when they are covered with snow. Then they live on the prairie and in the valleys at the foot of the mountains, and as I did not care to follow them into the mountains, I concluded to go back on the plains, and again try my luck on the buffalo.

# CHAPTER VIII.

IN KANSAS AGAIN—NOT A HAPPY FAMILY—
A THIEF NOT IN LUCK—EMIGRANTS ON A
HUNT—MORE INDIANS.

WHEN I left off deer hunting, I went back
about two hundred miles east on the Arkansas
River, not far from the head of Pawnee River,
in Buffalo County, Kansas. Here I hired
three men to go with me to haul the meat to
market. I could kill all the buffalo I wished
to, but the trouble had been for me to get it
to market. For this reason I hired these three
men—one of whom had a good team—to go
with me. They were no hunters, but they
suited me all the better for that.

We took up our headquarters on Alkali
Lake, and we had been out but a short
time when it became evident that my men
were not destined to dwell together in peace
and harmony, and I soon saw unmistakable
symtoms of a disruption. Two seemed to
have some kind of pique at the other, and were

continually imposing upon him, and were tak--
ing advantage of every occasion to taunt and
insult him. However, a l.ttle incident oc-
curred which prevented any shedding of blood.
although the one so crowed over had several
times threatened to kill the other two, and had
even asked me to loan him my gun, and had
supplied himself with cartridges for the purpose, and had not this little occurrence which I
am about to relate transpired, I think he
would have attempted their destruction.

We were out one day and I struck a large
herd of buffalo, and fearing that as I was likely
to have to take some violent exercise, my
pocket-book might work out of my pocket
and get lost, I handed it to the teamster to
hold for me while I was killing buffalo. He
said he would do so—I have never seen him
or the pocket-book since—and I went after the
herd. As soon as I was fairly out of sight he
jumped into his wagon and drove off. When
I returned to camp in the evening and found
him missing, I saw through the whole affair.
I told the two men left that the fellow had

robbed me and related the circumstance to
them, and they asked me to hitch my team to
the wagon and let them go after him. I
finally consented and took them to the nearest
railway station, and they, guessing the course
he was most likely to take, boarded the first
train and headed him off. They captured him
without difficulty and took him to Las Animas,
in Colorado. Here they took him before a
Justice, and one of them made oath that he had
stolen the team from them—although it was
his own—and proved it by the other. The
magistrate remanded him to jail, and turned
his team and wagon and my pocket-book over
to his captors, which they brought back with
them. The would-be thief lay in jail until
court set, when he was released, there being
no one to appear against him. Nevertheless,
it must be allowed that he paid rather dear
for his venture. What the other two did with
the team I can not say, as I lost sight of them
almost immediately afterward. I remained
here a few days, and went in to Sherlock with
a load of meat. There were a great many

emigrants there, most of them had good teams
and some were anxious to go out on a hunt.
I told them I would give them half the meat
for hauling it in, and there was no trouble in
finding persons ready to accept my offer.
They mustered up three teams and we started
out with ten men and three women, all inspired
with eager anticipation of something outside
of their usual line of life. We went out about
twenty-five miles and camped for the night.
While the men were preparing for the night
and the women getting supper I went and
killed a very large buffalo. They almost went
into ecstasies over it, and it was not long until
we had several nice slices of the tenderloin
fried and ready for distribution.

We moved on the next day, as the women
complained of the water, which was alkali,
and started to a good spring which was about
ten miles farther on. When we reached the
spring we discovered a band of Indians camped
near it. As soon as they saw us they picked
up and left their meat roasting on the fire.
We moved on to the spring, but I could hardly

get my folks to stay long enough to get a drink, they were so much afraid that the Indians would return and kill and scalp us all. They wheeled their teams about and started for Sherlock in a sweeping trot, and looking back every few minutes expecting to see an army of painted demons after them thirsting for gore and hankering for scalps. "O! what will we do if they do come?" they would say. "Kill 'em," I replied laconically, for I was vexed at their useless fright and did not exert myself very much to pacify them. However, we reached Sherlock in safety, and terminated the expedition without the loss of a single man, or woman either.

A short time after this I took a man with me went to my old hunting ground—the source of the Pawnee River. One day as we were driving along the bed of the river where the bluffs rose moderately high on either side, I looked down and saw a group of something which I took to be a herd of buffalo that had come in for water. I jumped from the wagon and ran down the draw toward them. I could only see the top of their humps, and I thought they were coming toward me. I ran on, and, all at once, I ran into a gang of squaws taking care of their horses. I then knew what my buffaloes were. They were Indians crawling up a small ridge which pointed down to the draw where I was. I saw that I was in a close place and got out as soon as I could. When I got back to the wagon and told him that what I took to be buffaloes were Indians, he looked frightened and asked if I thought there was any danger of them coming after us. I replied that if they did we could kill as many of them as they could of us. This seemed to be rather poor consolation to him, and he said that he could not see how that would comfort a dead man. While yet talking of the Indians I saw a herd of buffalo come in sight. We killed four and caught one calf. We then loaded our meat in the wagon and took it to to Pierceville, the nearest station. Here we found a company of soldiers looking for the Indians I had seen the day before.

# CHAPTER IX.

THE WAY SOLDIERS CHASE INDIANS—DRESS PARADE—A GREENY CATCHES A BUFFALO CALF—"HELP ME TO LET IT GO."

The soldiers mentioned in the preceding chapter had received a dispatch that eighty Indians had crossed the K. & P. railroad, near Monument station, evidently bent on mischief, and were ordered to overhaul them. They were commanded by Captain Payne, who asked me if I saw them. I answered that I had.

"When?" asked he.

"This morning."

"Where were they?"

"Out near the head of Pawnee River."

"Will you go with us to find them?"

"Do you want to take them some blankets?"

"No, by G—d; we do not. We have some pills for them, and if you are a good hand to prescribe them you can have a chance. Can you go?"

(10)

"I can; but I am tired of going after Indians under officers that won't let us hurt them, when we do go."

"Just try me once."

"Well, if you will promise to take no prisoners I will go, but if you want to take prisoners, count me out."

The Captain laughed and said "all right." He then ordered the men to mount. The word was soon given and we started, and within four hours were at the place where I saw the red skins. They were gone, but their camp bore evidence of having been deserted only an hour or so before. The trail showed that they had gone down the bed of the Pawnee River. The sun was then about two hours high, and we might easily have made ten or twelve more miles before dark, but the captain after looking around a few moments said, "Well, we will camp here to-night," which was equivalent to saying, "Well, we will give them a good chance to get away."

It was ten o'clock the next morning before we were ready to start. Then the captain brought his men out on dress parade, very much in the same style as if he were preparing to move on Richmond. He had a train of four six-horse teams, an ambulance and a surgeon. The latter, however, he was not likely to need, unless some of his men should get hurt on dress parade.

We marched down the river a few miles when we found it necessary to cross. Here we wasted four hours in digging the banks of the river down so we could get the wagons across. We had proceeded but a short distance after crossing the river when we struck a place which the captain thought would make a good place to camp. Here he ordered a halt, and said we would lay over the rest of the day as we might not find so good a place to camp as this. The next morning we came out on dress parade, and about ten o'clock resumed our march. We went about twenty miles down the river, and crossed back at the mouth of what is called Buckner Creek. On this creek we struck a beaver dam, above which the water was about eight feet deep. One of the soldiers dismounted, threw out a fish line and soon took a fine fish. This caused quite an excitement, and the captain said we would have a mess of fish. We turned our horses out and remained here until noon the next day, when, after going through the customary dress parade, we started for Fort Dodge, which we reached without the loss of a man, and without finding any use for the surgeon or the ambulance. Here I received my discharge—I had put in four days—and went back to Pierceville. This Indian chase is a fair sample of the manner in which the government troops out here hunt Indians. One old hunter is worth a dozen soldiers in an Indian chase any time.

When I got back to Pierceville one of my horses had been snake bitten and was not fit for use, but, as there were plenty of emigrants passing through, I found one whom I hired to take his team and go with me. He was about fifty years old, and had never seen a buffalo. Everything was new to him, and he saw many wondrous sights. We camped the first night on the head of Pawnee River, and the next morning started north to what is called Hackberry Creek, and in the evening near sun-down my companion suddenly said, "Laws! Look there." As he was a taller man than I was, he had the advantage of me in looking over the hill. I rose up in the wagon, and was not a little surprised myself to see a herd of about two thousand buffalo just over the hill and within gun shot. They were grazing quietly and had not discovered us. Taking my gun I slipped to the to top of the hill, and fired several times, killing two. After dressing one I went to the other, which was a cow, and lay about a hundred yards from the first. Her calf had lain down near her, and I told him to slip up behind the cow and catch it. "All right," said he, "and when I catch it, you must come up and help me." I told him that I would do so, and he got down on his hands and knees and crawled up close to the dead cow, but the calf saw him and getting up walked around the cow toward him. By this time I could plainly see that there was going to be some fun in that vicinity in a short time, and patiently awaited developments. I did not have to wait long. As the calf came around the cow he lay as flat on the ground as he could, expecting to catch it as soon as it came within reach, but, contrary to his expectations, when within about eight feet of him, it suddenly sprang upon him, and began goring and trampling him in a lively manner. As the calf was not large enough to seriously injure him, I remained a spectator and allowed them to fight it out unmolested, and even if I had desired to help him, I could not have done anything for laughing. After a little struggle and a good deal of bellowing for help, he managed to get on his feet and run. The calf followed him about a dozen feet, and then turned and again lay down by the cow. As soon as I could get through laughing, I went to work and we soon had the calf secured.

The next morning we went on trail of the herd, and about ten o'clock we came up with them going West toward Silver Lake, which was about twenty miles distant. We followed them with the wagon until two o'clock in the afternoon without being able to overtake them. The man with me began to despair and say "We won't get any of them." I told him if he would allow me to get on a good saddle horse he had with him, and let me manage it to suit myself, we would get plenty of them. He said he wanted us to get a good load of meat, and told me to take him. I mounted the horse and told him to follow slowly, so as not to frighten the buffalo, and galloped off toward the herd. I rode pretty brisk until I got ahead of them and picketed the horse, and, getting right in their course, lay down and waited. I did not fire until they were within thirty yards and opened on them with good effect. By the time my partner drove up I had ten killed. "Well, bless my life," said he, "that beats anything I ever did see." When we got them dressed they made a good load, and we started for Pierceville, reaching there about daylight, having travelled all night.

# CHAPTER X.

UNSUCCESSFUL HUNTERS—DANGERS OF THE
PLAINS—IN MISSOURI AGAIN.

AT Pierceville, I sold a large portion of
my meat to the emigrants, but some of them
would not buy, and said they were going out
and kill their own meat. They began to fix
up their guns preparatory to slaughtering all
the buffalo on the plains. I told them that it
looked very much as if I had just as well give
up hunting, as they seemed to be going to kill
all the game. They said for me just to wait
until they came in, and then I could joke if I
felt like it. I advised them to take teams
enough with them to bring in the meat and
not leave so much to rot on the plains. Four
of them, each with a pack horse, started in
the direction from which I had come, but did
not succeed in finding any meat. About this
time they began to want water, but, not
knowing where to look for it, could not find
any. I had started out shortly after they did

and went to Alkali Lake, fifteen miles from the head of Pawnee River, and as I was driving along near Dry Lake, I looked in the basin of the lake and saw a squad of men, about a mile off. They saw me about the same time and hoisted the signal of distress. As I did not halt they came hurrying toward me, waving their hats and calling to me to stop. When they were near enough they asked me if I had any water with me, as they were almost dying from thirst, not having seen a drop of water for three days. Several of their horses had given out, and they had been digging with their knives for water in the bed of Dry Lake. I pointed to a hill about a quarter of a mile off, and asked them why they did not go to a spring at t' e foot of the hill and get all the water they wanted. They wanted me to take them to the spring, which I did, and it was not long before they were swallowing cool, sparkling water by the quantity. They were really nearly starved to death, and I believe if I had not come along and helped them out they would have died

(11)

within half a mile of water. Men who are
unacquainted with the plains have no business
on them without a pilot. There are springs
that never go dry, but a person who did not
know their location might die within a few
steps of one. There are many persons
from the East who go out on the plains without a guide, and, not being acquainted with
the lay of the land, suffer exceedingly for
want of water, and some times even die from
thirst. Besides this, most emigrants, and persons from the East, who go out on the plains
for buffalo, come armed with squirrel rifles
and shot-guns, and if they were to find ever
so many buffalo it would be almost impossible
to kill them. True they might occasionally
get one with the squirrel gun, but it would be
a rare occurrence, and a man might work
with a shot-gun a year and then not get a
buffalo.

If any of my readers ever conclude to take
a buffalo hunt on the plains, they need not
start out by themselves with a rusty shot-gun.
and I would advise they to employ a pilot.

even if they have to pay him five dollars a day. A good pilot is indispensible for several reasons. In the first place, a novice, not knowing where to look or how to hunt, might wander over the plains for weeks and never see a buffalo, and even if he should find them, the chances are, that if left to himself, he would not be able to kill any. Another reason is the danger of suffering or even dying for water, for, while there are springs here that afford a barrel of water per minute, they are not so numerous, nor so conspicuously located as to make one at all liable to run into them.

When I returned to Pierceville I concluded to go to Missouri and spend a few weeks with my family. I reached home on the 13th day of June, 1876, and remained there until October, when, in company with my oldest son and a man named Baker, I started in a wagon for the plains again.

# CHAPTER XI.

ON THE PLAINS—A GANG OF BADGARS—
WOLVES—SCARED BY INDIANS—THE HORSE
AS A PICKET GUARD—SNOW BOUND, ETC.

WHEN we left Missouri we struck for the
Pawnee River—my old haunt, as the reader
by this time has doubtless discovered—and
after fourteen day's driving, reached our des-
tination in safety. We concluded to take up
our headquarters on Clear Lake, and when
within a few miles of the lake I saw a solitary
buffalo helping himself to the grass. As soon
as he saw us he took fright and ran. I had a
pony along, which I had taken in a fight with
the Cheyennes. So I mounted him and went
in pursuit. The pony was used to it and soon
crowded the buffalo so close that he turned for
a fight, but I shot him down before he got
too close, and was dressing him when they
drove up with the wagon. It was quite a wonder to them, being the first buffalo they had
ever seen.

One evening when we had stopped near Silver Lake, and camped in a small branch for the night, Baker, who happened to walk out a few steps from the camp, called me and said "Oh! look over there; what a gang of badgers." I went to him to investigate the badger business, and saw that it was a herd of buffalo just over the hill, with the tips of their humps just visible. I ran back and seized my gun and, slipping to the top of the hill, succeeded in killing twelve. These when dressed made us a good load, which we took to Sherlock and shipped. We then took up our abode on Alkali Lake. I left Baker to make a dug-out—a house dug in the bank of a branch or the brink of a hill—and went out about four miles where I found a dead buffalo with a number of wolves gathered about it. Wolf skins were bringing fair prices, and I told my son that we would put some strychnine in the carcass and camp close by and see the result. The next morning we went to see the effect of the poison, and found thirteen dead wolves. We skinned them and started to camp for the

wagon. We had gone but a short distance
when we stuck a large herd of buffalo coming
toward us on a run. I ran out and lay down
directly in their course, but held my fire until
they were within twenty paces when I opened
and fired about twenty shots while they were
passing, but only succeeded in killing six.
My boy was terribly frightened while they
were passing, as from where he stood it looked
as if they were running right over me, as he
could not see me lying in the grass, and it was
not until I began firing and the smoke raised,
that he was undeceived. We dressed the
buffalo I had killed and again started to camp.
As we were going along my son looked off to
the left and said, "Yonder is a man on horseback." He was coming toward us, and when
he was a little closer I saw that it was an
Indian. When I told my boy what it was
he began to cry and say he wished he hadn't
come, and so on. By this time several more
appeared in sight, which frightened him all the
more. I told him not to get scared, and
bringing my gun from my shoulder ordered

the foremost of them to halt, which he did.
I asked him what tribe he belonged to and he
answered "Omaha." I told him not to come
any closer, and he stood there naming over
several articles and jabbering generally. I
then asked him how many there were of them
and he said there were thirty, which was near
the truth, as I could see about that number.
He asked in turn how many there were of us
and I told him eight. He was directly between us and our camp, and I did not want
him there, so I told him to turn to the left as
some of the boys might want to shoot him if
they saw him. He turned and went around,
carefully watching for "the boys," but without
seeing them. I only wanted him out of my
way, so we could get back to camp.

They pitched their teepes on a hill about a
mile from our camp, as though they were
going to stay all night. As it was earlier in
the day than usual to prepare for camping for
the night, and as the place they selected was
on a hill instead of near water, it aroused our
suspicions and we began preparations for de-

fense. Their camping on the hill seemed very much as if they wanted to watch our camp. We expected that about day-break they would make an attack on us. As a precaution I picketed a horse on a knoll about a hundreds yards from camp to warn us before they were upon us, if they should come. The horse is about the best guard against surprise by Indians, being much superior in that respect to a dog. A dog makes too much noise entirely, while the horse only snorts at most, besides the horse does not sleep as much nor as soundly as the dog, and seldom allows himself to be surprised. If Indians are approaching no matter how slyly he is sure to discover it, and lets you know it by restlessness and uneasiness, loud sniffing or snorting.

We passed the night without any visit from the red skins. Our horse never showed any signs of alarm, but we watched him very closely until about nine o'clock in the morning. It was a very foggy morning and it was about ten o'clock before the fog cleared up so we could see. As soon as I could see I went out on a knoll and looked carefully in every direction, but could discover no trace of any Indians. Going back to camp I got my gun and some ammunition, and myself and my son went up on the hill, where the Indians had pitched their teepee the day before, and found that they had left. I examined closely to see which way they went, and soon discovered their trail leading toward White Woman Creek. I afterward learned that while on their way they came very nearly getting another fellow. He lived in a dugout, and was getting his supper when he saw them rushing toward him. He tried to make them stop, but as they paid no attention, he slammed the door shut and made it fast. The red skins gathered around the door and began to try to burst it in. As the door was not exceedingly strong, and the man inside thought he was sure to be killed any way, he began firing through the door at the Indians and brought several of them down. They soon gave up their plan of going through the door as a bad

(12)

job, and some of them got on the top of the house and began shooting down through, but they were no more successful here than at the door. The Indians will not fight if they can not do so without losing men. I heard the old chief of the Ogallahs say that it did not pay to give man for man, and that he wouldn't do it. One resolute and experienced man can hold fifty Indians at bay, if he has a good position and manages it correctly. These red skins, finding that they could not get their man without considerable loss, finally moved back about a half mile and stationed themselves on a small hill to watch the dug-out, that he might not escape before dark, when they would make another attack, and take him in. But, as soon as it began to get dark, he crept out and made his escape, but ran a very narrow risk. Although this poor fellow escaped from the Indians, he was soon overtaken by a worse fate, if a worse fate than falling into the hands of the red devils is possible. He and his two partners were out hunting and were caught in a snow storm and frozen to death, and their bodies nearly eaten up by wolves before they were discovered.

A short time after this myself and my son went out one morning and got after two buffalo cows, and followed them about twelve miles before we got them. We were then within about six miles of Silver Lake, and started for that point. It suddenly began to turn fiercely cold, and I began to expect a blizzard, so we hurried on toward the lake and our camp, and when about a mile from our halting place, and the sun almost down and the cold increasing, I saw, about a mile and a half to my left, a very large herd of buffalo. I think there must have been two thousand of them, and I was anxious to get at them, but as it was so frightfully cold and night was fast coming on, I told my boy we would go down to the spring and wait until morning, and then we would try what we could do for them. About the time we lay down for the night I noticed a very black cloud hanging in the north, but we made extensive speculations on the number of buffalo we were to get the

next morning, but when we waked up we
found the snow fully a foot deep, and
the air piercing cold, and the snow still falling.
The air was bitterly cold and I proposed to lie
still until the storm was over, but my boy
soon became tired and got up to kindle a fire.
In this he failed and soon commenced crying
because of the cold, and I was compelled to
get up and make a fire myself, which I succeeded in accomplishing after considerable
trouble. Our horses could not be found, as
they had gone off in search of shelter from the
storm, and Jimmy was crying to go to Sherlock, a distance of thirteen miles, so I was in
a rather queer position. I was almost afraid
to start to wade the snow to Sherlock, but
finally consented to try and make the trip.
When we got started we found it even colder
and more difficult traveling than we had expected. The snow was drifting everywhere
and the wind was blowing fiercely, driving
the snow through our clothing, and while the
heat from our bodies melted it, the piercing
cold froze our clothing stiff, and besides, walk-

ing through the snow knee deep was very fatiguing and wearisome. It was several hours before we succeeded in getting to the station, and when we entered a hotel a women met us at the door and asked if we were not frozen. I told her that we were all right and for her to prepare us something to eat. After we had eaten, she asked if I did not get very cold. I told her that I was colder then than I had been any time during the day. She then pointed to a red hot stove and told me I had better sit down near it and warm myself. I was not slow to act on her suggestion and soon had my feet almost against the glowing stove. I had not sat long until I discovered that there was something wrong with my feet. They first felt numb, but in a few moments they began to ache, and in a short time pained me so much that I could scarcely stand it. I went to bed leaving my socks on, but suffered so much with my feet that I could not sleep any, and the next morning my feet were almost perfectly black and swelled frightfully, and covered with blisters. There was no longer any mistake about the matter ; my feet were badly ·frozen, so much so that I could not walk for more than seven months. At the end of twenty days my feet showed strong symtoms of mortification, and I was put on a train and taken to Fort Dodge, a distance of sixty miles, for medical treatment. Here I employed a physician to attend me for two dollars a day. He burned off the dead flesh and scraped the buoe, and at the end of seven months I was able to walk a little, but was lame for a long time.

## CHAPTER XII.

ON THE PLAINS ONCE MORE—PLENTY OF GAME
—IN A BAD FIX—HE COULDN'T STAND THE
INDIANS—NOR LIGHTNING EITHER.

As soon as I was able I went to Sherlock and again started to hunting. I was scarcely able to walk, and would drive as near the herd as I dared and then get out of the wagon and crawl up within range.

Leaving Sherlock we (my son and myself) went west about twenty miles and, crosssing the Arkansas River, went south about thirty miles to Cimarron Creek, and, after following this stream about ten miles, I struck a big herd of buffalo. I succeeded in kliliug three, and we thought we would go in with them.

We went about ten miles on the road to the station and camped for the night. When we got up in the morning my boy went out after the horses, and had gone but a short distance when he whistled for me to look around, when I did so and saw a large herd of buffalo.

I took my gun, and, going out, lay down in
their course, and when they were close enough
I fired and killed one. The others gathered
around it and kept bellowing, and I kept firing
until I got nine. We dressed them and again
started on, but only made about five miles
that day, and again stopped for the night, and
the next morning, when we got up we found
one of the horses dead. I sent my son in after
a team, and he succeeded in finding one of my
old partners who was glad to help me out of
a scrape, and he came right out and hauled
my meat in for me.

I bought another horse immediately and
was again after buffalo, this time about forty
miles back on Cimarron Creek. We camped
the first night in the bed of a dry lake, and
slept in the wagon. In the morning when I
raised up I saw a herd of something about two
miles off, but could not tell whether they were
buffaloes or not, and asked my boy if he could
make them out. He began rubbing his eyes,
and, happening to turn his head in the opposite
direction, saw a herd of buffalo about a quarter

of a mile wide and fully a mile long, bearing right toward us, and nearly upon us. He called my attention to them as soon as possible, and by the time I could get my gun they were within twenty paces of us. We could distinctly feel the ground tremble as they galloped past, and during the time they were passing I put in good time shooting, and when they had gone by I had a good load, so we dressed them and again went in.

My boy then went back to Missouri, and I hired a man by the name of George Daniels for thirty dollars a month to go with me, but he only stayed three weeks, when the Indians scared him out, and he could not be persuaded to stay any longer. I sent him out one morning after the horses, and, when about a quarter of a mile from camp, he discovered a a couple of Indians making a charge on him. He came almost flying toward camp, screaming for help at every jump. I ran out to see what could be the matter, and the reds were right after him, but I persuaded them to stop, and he came up breathless from fright and

(18)

violent exercise. He thought that such adventures were frightful, and said he wouldn't stay for five hundred dollars a month. I told him that such little brushes were nothing when one got used to it. "But," he replied. "I would never get used to such. Why, here are snakes, lightning skunks, centipedes, tarantulas and Indians." I tried to console and reassure him, by telling him that if he wasn't born to be killed by an Indian he never would be, and if he was he couldn't escape it anyhow. But he said, "Born or not born, they would have gotten me if it hadn't been for you." I told him that unless it was God's will he would not have allowed them to hurt him, but he said he would rather depend upon me than God when the Indians were after him. But he was such a coward that I could not get any satisfaction from him, and I verily believe that his cowardice made his life a misery to him. It would be hard to find anything that he was not afraid of. One day as we were driving along we saw some antelopes near, and he asked me to let him take my gun and kill one.

There were plenty of antelope but I seldom tried to kill any, but he wanted to kill something, and I told him he could try. He was slipping along toward them very slyly, when, all at once, he turned and came running toward the wagon as hard as he could. When he came up I asked him what the matter was, and he said, "Didn't you see it lightning? I don't want any steel in my hands when it is lightning. Why, I have jerked many a knife out of my pocket and thrown it away on that account." I laughed and told him that if he wasn't careful he would get killed before his time yet. He didn't stay any longer, and as we got in to the station he went east, and I hired a fellow by the name of George Johnson, who was, if any difference, a bigger coward than Daniels. He stayed with me about twenty days, when he happened to an accident that caused him to leave. It happened in this wise: We had taken a load of meat in to the station, and were selling it out to the emigrants, of which there were a large number. Johnson struck up an acquaintance with some of them and was showing out to some young ladies, boasting of killing buffalo, riding wild horses and a great many things that he never did. While he was telling them how well he could ride, one of them said. "La, I wish you would ride one of Pa's horses. He throws nearly everybody off that tries to ride him."

Johnson said he could ride anything, he didn't care what it was, and some of the men saddled the horse and brought him out to Johnson  By the time things were in readiness for the show to begin, quite a crowd of folks of all ages, sizes and sexes had assembled to watch developments and to see the fun, and the wonderful feats of horsemanship. Johnson climbed into the saddle and told them to let the horse go.  They did so, and he began to rear and plunge in a fearful manner, and after a few jumps changed to the old trick of bucking and kicking.  All at once he jumped suddenly and stiffly on his fore legs, threw his head down to the ground and kicked as high as he could.  This was too much for the great horseman, and he went over the horse's head, with his arms, legs and fingers spread out for something to get hold of. As he went over, the seat of his pants caught on the horn of the saddle, and he left it behind him. He struck the ground on his all-fours, and, looking for the horse to be right on him, scrambled off on his hands and knees as fast as he could with that part of him, which, in a beef, is called the best steak, shining like a porcelain door-knob. He crawled along in this way for some distance, when finally he ventured to look back, and, seeing that the horse was not after him, he raised to his feet, and, gathering the back part of his pants in both hands, slunk away. It is hardly necessary to state that he did not come back to see the girls who saw him ride any more. He called on me the next morning and asked for his pay, and said he was going to leave the country, as he would never here the last of his ride if he stayed, and could never look into the faces

of the young ladies again. I told him not to
mind it as the horse had thrown everybody
that had tried to ride him. "But," he said,
"they never had their breeches torn off as I
had mine. It's no use to talk; I won't stay."
Being thoroughly convinced that I could not
prevail on him to remain any longer with me, I
paid him off and he went away, and I had to
look out for somebody to take his place.

# CHAPTER XIII.

WILD HORSES — THIRSTY AND HUNGRY —
WATER AT LAST—BONES ON THE PLAINS
—THE RESULT OF STRONGHEADEDNESS.

AFTER Johnson left me I ran across two
young men by the name of Stanfield and
formed a partnership with them. At that time
there were a great many wild horses in that
vicinity, and we concluded to try our luck
after them. So we started out and soon struck
a large drove, I think about seventy-five.
They were going west, and, as we had had
no experience in that particular line of hunting, we did not have any idea how far they
were likely to go, but followed them as closely
as we could, intending to get back that night,
but instead followed them about one hundred
and forty miles. As we had not intended any
such chase, we had made no preparations
for it and did not take any provisions with us,
and were compelled to do entirely without
food. I tasted no water at all on the first and

second days, and on the third day I came to a dry branch and got off my horse and began scratching in the mud for water. While thus engaged my horse jerked loose from me and started off across the prairie. I started after him, but he was soon out of my sight and I was left afoot and alone, having gotten separated from the others the day before. I was so thirsty that I tried chewing grass, and so weak that I could hardly walk. I gave up the chase and turned my whole attention to trying to get out of the scrape, and was doing my best to find water, but was so faint and weak that I could only make a short distance before having to stop and rest. I was dragging myself along in this manner when I saw a drove of wild horses ahead of me and coming nearly toward me. They kept looking back as if at something behind them, and I soon saw two men following them, and I began to make very emphatic signs for them to come to me. As soon as they saw me they came up to me and asked me what was the matter, but my tongue and throat were so dry and parched that I could not speak. It was one of the Stanfield boys and a man named Reece. They had no water but gave me some dried apples to chew, to create a flow of saliva to moisten my mouth, but it did no good. Stanfield then took me on the horse behind him and hurried off with me to a spring about ten miles away. It took us over an hour to get there, and I was very careful not to drink too much at once, but took about a pint and after waiting a few minutes, another, continuing in this manner until I knew there was no danger. It took a prodigious quantity to satisfy me, and it was two or three days before I got over my thirst. The horse that broke away from me died for want of water.

Many a man has gone out on the plains as I did, and died from thirst and hunger, or cold, and it is no uncommon thing to find their bones strewn over the ground where they have so perished. I have found many myself whose death doubtless came about in this way. I found one skeleton, the owner of which, had certainly frozen, as he had burned his wagon

(14)

and even his gun stock. He had died but recently, but the wolves had mangled his body beyond all possibility of recognition. Another whose bones I discovered had a bullet hole in his head, and, judging from the position of his gun, had evidently shot himself to put an end to his sufferings. Still another had his cloak wrapped about him, and had probably frozen or died from hunger and cold together, as there were no marks of violence on the body. These are only a few of the many instances I might mention, but of course a great many of the skeletons were those of Indians, but I could not distinguish them from those of whites. It is enough to know that they perished alone on the plains, and what their sufferings were no one knows.

My readers will see that it is much the safer plan, when persons are unacquainted. with the plains go out on them, to emply a good guide, and even then it will not do to take every one that offers himself, as there are plenty who profess to be acquainted with the country that know nothing about it, and a person would be as well off without them. I have helped several men out of bad scrapes that they had gotten into by trusting poor pilots, and would recommend everyone to be careful to get one that understands his business.

I remember once when I was hunting near Lakin Station, on the Atchison and Topeka railroad, and while there a couple of men asked me to pilot them across the country to the south of the Arkansas River. We soon struck a bargain and set out. I took a saddle horse with me, and they had a good team of mules. We traveled about twenty miles the first day, and camped at night on a small lake where there was plenty of water, and, when ready to start the next morning, I told them that they had better take some water along, as it was nearly twenty-five miles to the next water on our route. They had a barrel in the wagon, and I wanted them to put some water in it, but they said they could stand it, and besides the water would soon get warm and unfit to drink any way. So they contented themselves with drinking as much as they could, and

announced themselves ready to start, doubtless under the impression that would not get
thirsty any more that day. But in this way
they were sadly mistaken, for, as it was a
very hot day, and we were compelled to travel
in the broiling sun, about eleven o'clock they
began to want a drink, and would drive out
of the way to examine old dry lakes in the
hope of finding water. I told them that they
were only losing time and that the nearest
water was the lake I had spoken of, and that
we would get water sooner by driving directly
there, instead of wasting time in exploring
dry lake beds. They finally got angry and
told me that I did not know what I was doing,
and that they knew more about the country
than I did, and that there was no water within
forty miles of us. They got so incorrigible
that I told them that they might go to a
warmer country for all I cared and rode off
and left them. When I had gotten off a short
distance, I looked back to see if they were
following, but I saw that they had turned to
go back to Lakin. It was only about twenty

miles in a direct line and about thirty-five the way we had come, but to go directly there one must pass through a range of sand hills, which it is almost impossible to cross. They were in a hurry to get back, and thinking that they knew all about the country, took the direct line and ran straight into the sand hills, and, after traveling all that night and the next day, came out of the sand hills about thirty miles from the place they intended to strike. Here, however, they found water, but their mules had given out before they got through the hills, and they had left the wagon and walked the rest of the way, leading their mules, and when they had rested they gave a pilot five dollars a day to go back with them after the wagon, and all from thinking that they knew more than their guide.

# CHAPTER XIV.

NEW YORKERS ON A HUNT—NOT SO VERY
DEAD — NEW GAME — A REGULAR CHASE
AFTER WILD HORSES.

ABOUT the liveliest buffalo hunt that I ever
experienced happened in this way :   A couple
of New Yorkers went out west on business,
and having a few days of spare time concluded that they wanted to take a buffalo chase.
They had never seen a buffalo, but wanted to
very badly, and they thought they would like
to kill a few dozen too.   So one day, after
they had been talking to the landlord about
wanting to go after buffalo, he said he would
see me, as he thought I would go with them.
He accordingly came to me and asked what
I would charge to go.   I asked him how they
wanted to go, and told him if they proposed
to go on foot that I would rather be excused.
He said that if they went they would take a
two-horse carriage, and I agreed to go as
pilot for three dollars a day, and in a few

moments all arrangements were completed and we were on our way, the landlord joining us.

Crossnig the Arkansas River, we went about thirty miles south that evening, and camped for the night near the north fork of Cimarron River, and the next day, after driving about twenty miles, we struck game. We attacked a big herd and had a lively time with them for a while, and when the buffalo left the field we noticed four lying on the ground dead, or supposed to be so. When we approached them, one was lying on his back, and Potter, the landlord, remarked that we had "given that one h—l," but a little closer examination showed no blood, and further, the animal was breathing rather lively for a dead buffalo, and I rightly conjectured that he had been knocked into the ditch by the others and had been unable to get out, and I took the precaution to observe him from a point a few feet away, for I was expecting him to make a mighty effort and come out in a way that would make it unsafe to be too near him, and

I was right. Scarce a minute had elapsad. when, summoning all his strength he floun- dered, plungged and finally gained his feet and mad made quite a scatterment among his captors, who, however, recovered from their surprise in time to perforate him with bullets, and make him safely dead. During the racket the herd stampeded, and the horses becoming frightened mixed with them, and ran about three miles before they got clear and stopped. When the horses were brought back, Potter proposed that we make another dash on them, but I objected, as we already had more meat than we could take back with us and I did not like to see it wasted. He said he wanted to see one of the New Yorkers kill one anyhow, and the two went again after the herd, which by this time had begun to get together again, and in about for hours came back with thirty-six buffalo tongues. It an- gered me to see such a useless waste of meat, but they were proud of their achievement and didn't care for me. The two New Yorkers were enjoyed, and one of them said that he

wouldn't take a thousand dollars for his sport.
By they the time they returned I had the four
we had killed dressed, and we loaded up and
went back having been three days.

While out on this three days trip we saw a
great many wild horses, and happened to be
speaking of them to a bystander named Boslen,
who he began to get considerably interested,
and finally asked me what I would charge
to catch some for him.   I answered by saying
that I did not have a sufficient number of
saddle horses for such a chase.   He said that
he had plenty, and inquired how many I would
need, and proposed to furnish the saddle
horses and as many men as I wanted if I
would go, and offered me five dollars a day.
I told him that I did not wish to hire in that
way, for I might fail to catch any, and he
might perhaps think I did not try, but said if
he would be at all the expense and furnish me
six saddle horses and two good hands, and
give me five dollars a head for all I could
catch I would go, to which he readily agreed,
and we closed the bargain forthwith.   I then
(15)

chose six horses from his stable and we
made preparations for the chase, and were
soon on our way. We found several herds
before we struck one that suited us. The herd
we finally concluded to capture one that I had
seen a great many times when I was out after
buffalo, and I was well acquainted with their
range. We went as close them as we dared
and after carefully examining them by the aid
of field glasses, my employer, Boslen, said
that they would do. The next thing to do
was to fix the camp as near the centre of their
range as possible, as wild horses, when chased,
seldom or never leave their range, though this
may somtimes contain hundreds of square
miles, and it is necessary to know the range
and place the camp near the centre, in order
that fresh horses horses for the chasers may
be ready any time they happen to pass near
the camp. I told Boslen where to fix the
camp and announced my intention of starting
the herd early the next morning. The point
I selected for our base of operations was an
old and well-known camping place on Cimar-

ron River, about thirty miles west of where we then were. This I chose as the most suitable place because it was near the centre of the range of our game, and because there was plenty of good water there, whereas in most places the lakes had nearly gone dry and what little water that was left was going. So next morning Boslen and the two men started to the camping place, and I started for the wild horses. I was mounted on a good horse and rode up to the herd. When I was within about a half mile of them they saw me, and while some would elevate their heads and watch me very, while others would stick their tails straight up into the air, and taking a long, high trot would circle around among the others and snort. But I rode on, and the whole herd finally began to circle around me snorting, and occasionally one would stop to get a better look at me, and after satisfying himself would snort loudly and move on with the rest. I sat perfectly still on my horse and waited for them to move off, which, after making a half dozen circles, they did, going west toward the place where I had told Boslen to fix our headquarters. When they struck out I followed them as fast as I could, but could only keep in sight and had a good horse to ride too. Shortly after they started they struck a wagon road called the Doby Wall Trail, and following it passed close to our headquarters, where I wanted to change horses, but I knew that the others were not there yet and I followed on. My plan was to chase them down and capture the whole herd. We might have chased them awhile and then dashed into them and lassoed a few, but I concluded to keep up the chase until they were chased down. As the wild horse gets tired he gets less wild, and by having suitable headquarters so that one can change his horse without giving them much rest, the whole herd can be caught.

This herd passed near our proposed camp and went on west to the line between Kansas and Colorado, here they turned to the south and kept this course until they struck the south fork of Cimarron River, when they turned east, passing our camp again again, this time on the south. I took advantage of this opportunity to change horses, and was again after them with more vigor than before. They went on east near the place where I started them. Here I saw two men who had been lost two days, and could not find their way out, as the sky was cloudy, and they could not keep their course. They said they were nearly starved and would like something to eat. On the frontier it is customary to divide, as long as you have any thing to divide, and I gave them a biscuit apiece, half of what I had, told them which way to go, and went on after my horses The herd did not seem disposed to go any where near the camp, but played back and forth across the country between Wild Horse and White lakes. This did not suit me, as my nag was getting fagged and I was afraid I would have to go all the way to camp to change. This I did not like to do, as it would give them a chance to rest, and I would consequently lose nearly, or quite, all I had accomplished in two days hard work. However, as

good luck would have it, I ran across a cow-
boy, and gave him five dollars to go to camp
and tell them to meet me with a fresh horse
on the old Santa Fe trail, and I was again in
pursuit of my horses. They were getting tired,
and almost directly after I left the cowboy
they struck out nearly toward camp, and I
stayed within ten miles of the camp that night,
and the next morning very early I started to
intercept the men who were to bring the horse,
and struck the Santa Fe trail just in the nick
of time. There I got a fresh horse and some
grub, and as soon as possible was chasing my
wild horses. I found them near the place
where I had left them, and most of them were
lying down. They have wonderful endurance, which the reader will perhaps understand when I state that that night one of the
mares gave birth to a colt which traveled with
the rest all the next day, until about an hour
by sun in the evening, when I halted for the
night, knowing that the herd would stay there
with the colt. By this time I had them so
worried and cowed that they grazed all around

me in the night, and when I waked the next
morning, they were nearly all lying down,
stretched out like dead.   When I started them
they moved off very slowly, being very stiff
and sore, in a westerly direction, and I followed them again into Colorado, when they
took nearly the same route as before, turning
south and then east and coming back into
Kansas, and when I again stopped for the
night I was within about a half mile of camp,
but it was cloudy and so dark that I could not
see the camp, though I knew I was near it,
but was surprised when I waked up in the
morning to find myself so much nearer
than I expected.   I found the boys all
asleep, but soon waked them up and got a
fresh horse and more grub and went back to
see about the herd.   This time I took one of
the men with me to take care of the colt
when it should give down, which I knew
would not be long.

When I started the horses this morning
they were so tired and stiff, as to be nearly
docile and I was able to drive them nearly as

I chose. So I drove them about to suit myself that day, and at night had them back near
camp. We turned the colt out with them,
and I told Boslen that we would start for
Lakin Station with them the next morning,
but when morning came I concluded to drive
them around before we undertook to drive
them in, and when we did start in with them
we took a direct line for the station, and
crossed the sand hills. We were two days
crossing them, during which time the horses
got no water at all, but as soon as we were
over them we struck a lake and they drank to
repletion, from the effects of which eight of
them died, and I lost forty dollars. We then
drove them about twelve miles to a cow
corrall, where we corralled them, closed them
in, and drove them across the river to Lakin,
safely housing the twenty-four head.

## CHAPTER XV.

AFTER WILD HORSES AGAIN — INDIANS — A
BIG DRIVE—A CLOSE BRUSH WITH INDIAS.

MY good luck in this chase inspired me to
try it again. I wrote to Missouri for my son
and son-in-law to come out and help me, and
in the meantime I allowed the saddle horses
to rest and recuperate. They arrived in a few
days and we started out, again south of the
Arkansas River. When we arrived in the
region of Wild Horse Lake, we found that it
had rained very heavily, and the lakes were
all full, so I told the boys to establish the camp
about ten miles west of Wild Horse Lake, and
I started a drove of seventy-two horses. I
drove them twelve days, but at the end of that
time found that we were nearly out of provisions, and told the boys that one of them must
go back to the station for more. While he
was preparing to start I discovered a herd of
buffalo, and told them to put the horses to

(16)

the wagon and I would get a load of meat for
them to take in with them. As we were
going out after the buffalo, I discovered a band
of Indians about three miles off and coming
toward us. My son was just starting to get
a young antelope that he saw, and I beckoned
for him to come up, as I did not know whether
the Indians were friendly or not, and wanted
to be ready in case of an emergency. When
he came up I showed them the Indians, and
told them that it was possible that we might
have to fight, and for them to keep cool and
not get excited. I told them to get all the
ammunition together and I would go out
toward them and find out how the land lay.
I went a few hundred yards toward them, and
took a position where I could watch their
movements. They came down into the creek
bottom, which was about a mile wide, and
were out of my sight for some time, and in
the interim I changed my position so that I
could see them as soon as they emerged from
the bottom. When they again came in sight
they were about half a mile from me, and

seemed amazed at seeing us. They halted and gathered in a close group, and seemed to be holding a consultation. I signalled to learn what tribe they belonged to, but they paid no attention to me. I then signalled to know if they were friendly and what they wanted, but received no reply. I then went back to the wagon and told the boys that they meant no good, and ordered the ammunition placed where it would be most convenient. By the time we had things in readiness, the Indians had formed and were ready to make a dash on us. As soon as they started I lay down and levelled my gun to drop the foremost, but he saw my intention, and, whirling his horse about, dashed back. The next followed him, and the next in like manner, until the whole band were out of range, when they again stopped and held another council. I stood up on the wagon to watch them, and saw that they were preparing to surround us. The hill was in the shape of a half circle, and their plan was to go around the back of it, where we could not see them until they got around. So

I told the boys to get ready and get to the top
of the hill as fast as they could, as the Indians
meant to surround us, and we must get to the
top to intercept them. I sprang on the saddle horse and left them to come up with the
wagon, and dashed to the top of the hill,
where I could see the whole game of the
Indians. They were coming around the hill
stationing one of their number about every
hundred yards, and would have been all
around us in a few moments. I sprang from
my horse and crawled up where I could see
over the crest of the hill and could have picked
one off every shot. But they saw me and
knew that they were beaten, and whirled suddenly around, and, lying flat on their horses,
beat a hasty retreat, and did not stop until
entirely out of sight. We did not leave that
night, but picketed our horses and remained
until morning, for I knew that they would not
attack us any more that night, though the
boys thought sure that we would get our hair
lifted before daylight. The boys were afraid
to go in by themselves in the morning and I

had to go in with them, and, after laying in a
good supply of provisions, we started out again
to gee what had become of my wild horses.
We found them without any difficulty, and I
again started them. This time I followed
them, with several little ups and downs, for
fifteen days, at the end of which time they
were docile enough that I could drive them
almost as I chose.

Thinking that they were about ready to
drive in, I drove them near the camp one evening, and then next morning got one of the boys
to help me and we started them toward the
station. I had had a long chase and my
saddle horses were considerably jaded, and
when within about thirty-five miles of the
station, I found it necessary to go in and get
some fresh horses. So I left the boys to
manage as well as they could and mounted
the freshest horse, and procuring three fresh
horses, hastened back and found them just a
little nearer than when I had left them. We
had good luck until we attemped to corrall
them, to get them across the river. They

were afraid to go in the corrall and we could not persuade them in any way to do so, and we finally gave it up and swam them over the river. I was a little afraid of the experiment, but it worked all right, and I drove sixty-nine head of horses into the station the next day. This was a good haul, but catching wild horses is not by any means desirable work, and does not pay as well as one would suppose, as it is a long, hard job to capture a herd, and they are generally small and scrawny at that, and sell at almost nothing.

This was my last wild horse chase for the season, as it suited me much better to hunt buffalo than run wild horses, and I got a contract to furnish meat for the hotels and went out after buffalo.

I hired a man by the name of Black to go with me, but the Indians were so troublesome that he only remained with me a few days, and I hunted by myself. I established my camp on the Pawnee River, right on the old Indian trail, and went to work to get some meat. The first night I stayed alone I began to have fears of the Indians, and during the night this fear grew upon me so much that it was impossible for me to dismiss them from my mind. I did not sleep at all that night, and the next morning I was up bright and early preparing to shift my quarters. I went back from the river about three miles on the flats, but still on the trail. I stopped here but a short time, as I did not feel much safer than where I was, and hitched up again and drove to the top of a hill about a mile and a half farther on. Here I halted and looked around to see what I could see, and discovered something moving toward me a couple of miles to the northeast. I at first thought they were buffalo, but in a moment I saw that they did not move like buffalo. While watching them they went out of sight and soon reappeared again, which satisfied me that they were not buffalo. When they were nearer me I saw that they were men, and mounted, and I then knew that they were Indians moving right toward me, and I began to make preparations to give them a warm reception.

The most suitable spot for a fight that I
could see was an elevated place about a quarter of a mile to my left.   Here I posted myself and commenced filling my empty cartridges.   The Indians were fast getting nearer
and it seemed to me that I never made as
slow progress in filling cartridges before, and
yet I was working as for dear life.   However,
there were only six of the red skins, and I
knew that with anything like a fair show I
could take care of myself.   When they were
about two hundred yards off, I rose to my feet
and waved my frying pan toward them, and
no sooner did they see it than they raised the
yell and dashed toward me.   I motioned to
them to stop, but they paid no heed and came
dashing on.   I dropped on one knee and
resting my elbow on the other levelled my
gun at the foremost.   At this they whirled
with their horses sideways to me and turned
their saddles on the farther side and kept
themselves where I could not see them at all.
As they hung on the farther side of their
horses they would occasionally peep over their

horse's withers to see what I was doing and watching for a chance to rush upon me unawares. In this relative position we remained for some minutes, when they slid off their horses on the opposite side, taking care to keep their bodies protected by their ponies, but watching me intently all the while. Still holding my gun in position to cover any one of them in an instant, I asked them what tribe they belonged to, but they only answered "Yah." I said "Shriam," but they still answered "Yah." Again I asked, "Are you Ogallahs, Arrapahoes, Utes, or what?" but still they answered as before. I then took my gun from my face, but still held it in a position to do quick shooting, when they began to separate and move to the right and left, evidently intending to surround me. I motioned to them with my gun, to stay together, when they made signs to the effect that they wanted something to eat. I was afraid that this was only a trick to get me off my guard, but I moved cautiously toward the wagon, at the same time watching them very narrowly, to

(16)

catch any suspicious movement on their part.
Scarcely had I started toward the wagon than
one of them made a rush toward me, but I was
watching him, and turning suddenly around
stopped him effectually. The last act of his
life was to cover his face with his hands and
cry out "ow, ow, ow." I then motioned for
the rest to come to him, so that I would have
them close together and could cover them
easily with my gun. They came forward,
leaving their guns hanging on their saddles, in
pretence of friendship. When within about
about fifteen paces I ordered them to halt,
which they did, but expressed a desire to shake
hands with me, and kept saying "How, how,
how." I found it rather a delicate affair to
manage, as they could, if they chose, have
taken me in, but they were sure that some of
them would pay the penalty with their lives,
and they did not care to make an open
attack, and wanted to get me at a disadvan-
tage, and, while I could have readily shot
one or more of them down, I was afraid to do
so, because I did not know what effect it would

have on the rest. It might so frighten them
as to make them leave in a hurry, but it might
exasperate them and cause them to rush right
upon me and overpower me, which they
could easily do should they take a notion to
do so. It was the most trying time I ever
experienced, and I held them in this manner
for more than an hour, when they gave up the
hope of getting to shake hands with me, and
began to try to steal back to their guns, but
when one would make a move toward his
horse I would instantly cover him and order
him back into the squad. My attention was
called to one who acted as if he did not know
I was anywhere near, and was doing his best
to assume a careless air, and seemed to be
carelessly twirling a lariot which he held in
his hand. After swinging it round a while, he
arrarently let it loose accidentally, and one end
of it fell almost at my feet. After letting it lie
for a moment he began winding it up, but
instead of drawing the rope toward him, he
was following it toward me as he wound it
up, but I understood his plan, and stopped

game and his existence about the same time.
I then brought my gun to bear on the rest
who sprang on their horses and hurried away.
I watched them until they disappeared about
two miles off.

The same day that I had a brush with the
Indians, the same band ran across a man
named Matthews, and two men who were
driving a herd of cattle, and by appearing very
friendly succeeded in throwing the men off
their guard. They approached them in a
friendly manner, and, after shaking hands with
them, called for something to eat—an Indian
is always hungry—and partook liberally. But
they were only watching for an opportunity,
and no sooner did it appear than they shot two
of them down. Matthews sprang on his horse
and dashed away in time to save his life, but
was badly wounded in the shoulder by a shot
sent after him as he was fleeing for his life.
This will show my readers how treacherous
is the red man of the forest, and how little confi-
dence can be placed in his professions of sincere
friendship. I never saw one yet that it was

safe to trust, and I believe that my suspicions in this direction have several times saved my life. I have seen but very few Indians that were not dangerous and they were dead.

Immediately after this I went across to Silver Lake to join an old hunter who was camped there, as I did not like to be alone while the Indians were so troublesome. Besides, he was, as I have said, an old hunter, and in a scrimmage with red skins his equal was hard to find. Many an Indian had dropped at the crack of his rifle and he was well known among them, and was as universally feared as he was known. With him, and ten minutes notice, we could have made it warm for any number of reds likely to attack us, but when I came to his camp, I found that he had gone in to the station and I was compelled to stay by myself at last, with the Indians passing nearly every day. However, I continued hunting for some time without molestation from them, but succeeded in getting into some scrapes not much more agreeable than an Indian fight.

One day when I was out hunting the weather became cloudy and a cold rain set in which lasted two days and nights, completely soaking my blankets and chilling me nearly to death. Finally the clouds broke away and the rain ceased, and I went out for game. After going about four miles I saw two very large buffalo, and, slipping as close as I dared, shot one as it lay, and, while the other was examining it to see what ailed it, brought it down too. The weather was still cold for October, and it had clouded over again and was beginning to snow. I turned out my team and dressed the animals I had killed and, laying them with their backs nearly together, spread my blankets over them. I spread the green hides over that with the hairy side down, and then crawled in between the hides and blankets and lay there until the snow storm was over, which was two days, only coming out occasionally to get something to eat. While lying there the buffalo came all around me, and when it cleared away I got out and began to scatter them. I killed two and after dre⸺

ing them I put the four into the wagon. By
this time the snow was melting rapidly and it
was late in the evening. I drove over to the
place where I had camped during the rain
storm. I discovered when I arrived that a
band of Indians had camped there during the
snow storm and had but recently left. It was,
a narrow escape, but as the old saying goes
" a miss is as good as a mile," and I did not
get frightened after the danger was all over.
This spring was a noted camping place, being
right on a much used Indian trail, and was
used by white men as well as red skins. I
thought I might find some game farther on
and drove several on several miles, but, not
finding anything, concluded to drive in with
what I had. As I passed the spring on my
return I saw a squad of red skins camped
there again, but, as I had no occasion to stop,
passed by, within half a mile of them. If
I had been as thirsty then as I have been
many times, I most certainly should have
stopped, but the snow was melting and I could
get all the water I wanted without fighting

for it. When I was about a mile from their camp, I saw three buffalo lying with their backs toward me, but I did not know whether to kill them or not, as I already had four, and besides, the Indians had not yet seen me, and the report of my gun might rouse them and get them after me, but the temptation was too strong, and driving as near as I dared I took my gun and began to slip along toward them. When I was about close enough I looked to the left and saw three Indians stealing up on the buffalo that I was. They had not discovered me and I stopped and was watching them, but in a short time they discovered me. I straightened up and we stood for some moments watching each other, but I soon got tired of that, and again advanced on the buffalo, keeping an eye on the Indians as I did so. As soon as one of the buffalo got on his feet, I shot him down. The others sprang up and seem surprised that the one I had shot was lying down, but in less than a minute I had them also. I then got my wagon, and putting it between me and the red skins, who remained in the same place, proceeded to dress them, but closely watching the Indians, who, shortly after I began skinning my game, sat down on the ground and looked at me until I got through, when I loaded them on the wagon and drove off.

When I got in to Sherlock station I found a great excitement about the Indians, and the people supposed that they had killed me as I had been out so long. This was about the time General Custer and his command were killed by them. Uncle Sam had fed and fattened the red devils until they were in good fighting trim, and they went at it, and were killing people every day. About fifty were killed in the vicinity of where I was. They surprised the people at different places, almost before they were known to be anywhere near, and shot them down like wild beasts. Some were tortured and mutillated in the most revolting manner, and scalped and left to die. At one place a band of them surprised a school that was taught by a lady teacher, and captured the whole school. They did not kill

(18)

any of them, but satisfied themselves with frightening them nearly to death. They thumped and banged them about, and made as if they would tomahawk them, and pulled their hair and laughed when the frightened girls begged for their lives. Three young ladies of the school were stripped entirely naked and told to go home in that condition. After they had satisfied themselves with the pupils they started off, but the people had risen, and not half of those devils ever saw Sitting Bull again. But they stole a great many horses and cattle, and the cow-boys joined in pnrsuit. The cow-boys were more than a match for the reds, and took especial delight in fighting them. The troops finally came to the relief of the people, but they nearly always move too slow to catch Indians.

In this raid, however, Col. Lewis did good work, but was killed with several of his men, in an engagement on White Woman Creek. When this happened I was hunting on the same creek, but did not take much part in the fighting, as I thought that if the government fed and fattened the Indians for fighing, and kept soldiers to kill them when they were fattened, they might go ahead and do it. But while I did not take an active part in the hostilities, my occupation brought me in frequent collision with the redskins, but all the fighting I did was merely a pure matter of self defense, and I made it a point not to get into any unnecessary conflict with them.

One evening, a few days after the fight on White Woman's Creek, I saw a bunch of something in a side draw of the creek, and supposed it to be buffalo, but it was so smoky that I could not distinguish what it was, and went nearer. We were then within about a half mile of them, and, on going closer, I brought my field glass to bear on them and found they were Indians. They were lying on the ground holding their horses, which I regarded as rather suspicious, and was afraid that they had scouts stationed between me and them. I had with me at that time a man by the name of Brank Howard, and I told him that we would withdraw a few hundred yards to a ravine, or washout, to stay all night. This was a good position and afforded us a fair opportunity to repel any attack they should make. We hurried our supper all we could and as soon as possible put the fire out, so that it would not betray our position, and put ourselves in as good condition for defense as we could, when we sat down to watch and wait. Shortly after dark our dog began to bark and run savagely down the washout and then back, keeping up an incessant growling and barking, and we knew that the reds were prying around our camp with no good intent. Soon he grew more furious, and, after dashing about fifty yards down the ravine, he would come back with his tail between his legs as if frightened. This is the way a dog acts when Indians are about, and we expected to be attacked all the time, and kept ourselves in readiness to go to work in a second's notice. It was so dark and smoky that I never got to see them once, and after about two hours they went away, the dog became quiet, and Howard and myself took turn about sleeping

and watching during the night. · I examined
the ground around our camping place as soon
as I could see in the morning and found that
they had been within twenty paces of us.
These were a remnant of the band that had
the fight with Lewis a few days before, and I
suppose, perhaps, that the reason they did not
attack us was, that they were dodging the
sodiers and were in a hurry to get out of the
country.

The whites were not the only ones that
suffered during the trouble, for the Indians
were compelled to undergo some rather severe
privations. I remember the case of an old
squaw and a papoose about seven years old.
When the Indians were scattered in the fight
on White Woman, this squaw and child could
not get away, and, to avoid being taken by the
soldiers, hid themselves in a washout, and
when the soldiers left did not know which way
to go, as the tribe was scattered and broken
up, so they remained where they were. They
could get plenty of water, but nothing to eat,
except the carcasses of the animals that had

been slain in the fight, and so severe was their hunger, and so long did they remain there, that they had eaten one mule nearly up, the flesh of which, when they were found, was putrefied and smelled horribly, and the squaw and child smelled but little better. They were carried prisoners to **Ft. Dodge.**

## CHAPTER XVI.

### ENGLISHMEN ON A LARK.

Not very long after the occurrences mentioned in the preceding chapter, five Englishmen came to Lakin Station on a lark. They were not peers of the realm, neither were they dukes or baronets, but they were regular built, right lordly Englishmen, of the pure blood and true type, and were on a sight-seeing tour over this country. They had plenty of money with them, and I should judge from the way they scattered it right and left, that there was plenty more where that came from. They were seeing their fun and were paying for it too. They arrived at Lakin fully resolved to take a buffalo hunt on the plains.

They had the best of guns, each having a good rifle and shotgun apiece. They asked me what I would take to pilot them out on the "range" and I answered that if they were going to do the shooting that I would go as a pilot for five dollars a day. They said they would give it, and remarked that the price was cheap enough. The next day they procured a two-horse carriage, and, after laying in a full stock of ammunition and provisions, we started. I did not ride in the carriage, but took my wagon and team, so that I would be ready when they got tired of paying five dollars a day. When we left Lakin we started in a northeasterly direction. When about twenty miles out we ran across a large rattlesnake, which they thought was wonderful. As they wished to see all about it, I made it sing for them, and when I finally killed it, one of them had me to skin it to make him a hat band. Then they all had to take a swig of beer, of which they had brought a goodly quantity, which emptied one bottle. They then made a bet as to who could break the bottle while flying in the air, and began tossing the bottle up into the air and firing at it. Finally one of them succeeded in hitting it, and they all got into the carriage and we again started on. We had gone but a short distance when one of them, who had his head sticking out of the carriage, exclaimed "Law, look there," and called for the driver to stop the carriage. I thought he saw a buffalo or something of the kind, and began to look around for it, but failing to see any, I looked at him to see which way he was looking, and saw that he was almost going into hysterics over a large specimen of terrapin. They all clambered out and took a good look at it, turned it over with their guns and shoved it about with their boots until they were satisfied, then they drank another bottle of beer, made a bet as to who could hit it in the air, and when it was finally broken they got into the carriage and we again drove on.

We had gone perhaps a mile when four antelopes came dashing past us at full speed. All five of them jumped out with their guns and began firing at them as fast as they could. They were about the most excited set of men I ever saw. They fired about fifty shots and the poor antelopes ran for dear life, badly scared but not seriously injured, and I sup-

(19)

pose not much more excited than the Englishmen. The men were sadly disappointed at
the escape of their game, but consoled themselves by drinking anot⁻er bottle of beer and
breaking the bottle a before. We moved on
a couple of miles and camped for the night on
a small creek, and when we arose in the
morning we could see antelope in every direction, but we hitched up and drove on. The
antelope seemed to be tolerably tame, and the
pleasure hunters kept up a continual firing at
them as we passed along until after noon, but
without any other effect than to frighten the
animals. When we stopped for dinner one of
them suggested that they put "the old man"—
meaning me—to shooting or we would starve
before we could get back to the station.
"Because," said he, "we have fired five
'undred shots to-day and kille⁻ nothing, hand
if this thing is kept hup we will soon be out
of hammunition hand no game heither." They
then put it to a vote and it was unanimously
agreed that I should kill them an antelope. I
told them that if they would all stay in the

carriage I would try, and I thought perhaps
that we might have antelope for supper.  Long
before we got to our camping place I saw a
drove of antelope and got quietly out of the
wagon, slipped up as close to them as I could,
for I did not want to miss after poking so
much fun at the markmanship of the others,
and when close enough to shoot I lay down
in the grass and waited for "a good chance."
In a moment I got two in range and fired
bringing both of them down at the first shot.
At this the men leaped out of the carriage and
came running up to me, more excited, if possible, than when they fired the fifty shots at the
four scared antelope.  After allowing them to
thoroughly examine the first dead antelopes
they had ever seen, I took the entrails out,
threw the carcasses in the wagon and the
procession moved on.  The Englishmen still
kept firing at antelopes, badgers, hawks and
everything they saw.  This was kept up until
we reached Clear Creek, where we camped
for the night.  Here we found ducks almost
in swarms, and my friends got among them

with their shotguns and killed several of hem.
and we had a regular feast of antelope and
duck for supper.

In the morning we harnessed up again and
started in a northwesterly direction and traveled until we came to Bear Creek, where we
once more camped for the night, and in the
morning moved on again. When we had
gone about a mile we discovered fine buffalo.
These were the finest we had seen on the trip
and the English gentlemen were very anxious
to kill them all, and jumped out of the carriage and started boldly toward them, very
much as if they thought the buffalo would be
glad to see them, but when they were within
about a quarter of a mile of them the buffalo
raised their heads, and, taking a short look,
galloped off, leaving the nabobs sadly disappointed. When they complained of their bad
luck to me I told them that they had done
much better than I expected, as I thought they
would frighten them away before they got
half so near. They gave the buffalo up rather
reluctantly and kept up a continual firing at

antelopes and fowls as we traveled along until night, but with their usual luck. We camped for the night on a small creek called Rocky Branch, and in the morning while eating breakfast one of them said, "Mr. Youngblood, how much do we owe you?" I told him that I had been with them five days, and at five dollars a day it would make twenty five dollars. They paid me the money and said, "We are done hunting, and want to see you shoot a little." I told them that it was all right, and if they would stay with me awhile I would probably shoot something. We moved about six miles to White Woman Creek, where I struck a large herd of buffalo. I killed one the first fire, and got a "stand" on them and killed seven. We dressed them and moved on. As we passed along I kill four antelopes. When we stopped for night I cooked some of the buffalo humps. and my English lords thought it the finest meat they ever tasted. I had a good deal of fun out of them on account of their shooting. I told them that they had had me five days for twenty-five dollars and got nothing, and in one day I had made twice that amount. We drove back to the station, and there we had some more of the humps cooked for dinner, but my friends did not like them as well as they did my cooking out on the range.

The next day I bade my English friends farewell, and with the man Howard, mentioned before, again struck out for the range. At White Woman Creek I struck a large herd of buffalo, standing in the creek drinking, but before I could get close enough to shoot they started out, and I fired on them at long range, killing a large cow. She was just going up the bank, and when I struck her she came rolling down toward the water. She rolled off the bluff bank, about twelve feet high, and struck in thin mud and went most entirely under. Howard and I worked some time trying to get her out, but so deep was she in the mud that we could not move her. So we gave it up as a bad job and went on after the rest of the herd. I fired several shots at them but only breaking the shoulder of a calf about

six months old.   It could not keep up with
the rest and we followed it along up the bed
of a "side draw," until finally I saw that the
herd had stopped farther up the draw.   The
calf had gotten tired by this time and very
gentle, and I could easily have shot it, but I
did not want to frighten the herd, so we
headed it off and began to try to catch it.   I
could get tolerably close to it, but not close
enough to catch it.   It was small and I thought
it could not hurt me much, and when I would
let it pass me it would make at me for a fight.
I supposed I could push it off when it got to
me and stood my ground, and it came bowing
and shaking its head, and when within a few
feet of me made a big dash right at me like
an old ram, and before I could do anything
knocked me down and began trampling me
into the ground.   Finding that it did not mean
to let me up, I reached up and got it by the ears
and after quite a tussle got it down and finished it with my knife.   As soon as we could
dress it we started on after the herd, but had
to follow them about twelve miles before I

could get a shot at them to suit me. Here I shot one and it ran on about three hundred yards on a hill and fell. This was on Beaver's Creek, and the beavers had built a dam across the creek, so that we could not across with the team and wagon, and, as it was about sun-down, I told Howard to turn the horses out and I would go over and skin the buffalo. I crossed the creek on a beaver dam, and had hardly began dressing my game when I noticed three men about three quarters of a mile off on horseback and coming toward us. I took them to be Indians and told Howard to gather up the ammunition and get it handy as the Indians were coming, and I picked up my gun and started back to the wagon. But it was a false alarm, as the men were cow-boys looking up some lost cattle.

I had noticed that Howard did not seem to be in an easy frame of mind, any of the time he was with me, and I supposed that he had gotten into trouble somewhere and was dodging. I continually met men of this class out there and soon learned to think but little of it, and let it pass without any remarks or inquiries. I had not said a word to Howard, but noticed that, as we prepared to start in with our load, he grew more nervous and ill at ease than ever, and seemed to be extremely anxious and uneasy. In fact he was so much so that I thought it would be right for me to speak to him about it and give him a chance to unload himself to me, as it would be likely to relieve the strain upon his mind. So the first opportunity that offered I asked him if something was not troubling him, and if I could do anything for him. He then said with a sorrowful smile, "Do I act as if something was bothering me?" "I have seen many a man in your condition," answered I, "and can guess pretty well as to the cause; and if you are in a difficulty, and half way innocent, I will try to help you in some way or other, and if you are really guilty of some infernal crime I will agree not to give you away, so spit it out, and we will see what can be done. My opinion is that you got away with some fellow where you came from, but whatever it is let's

(20)

have it." He looked at me for a moment as
if amazed, and finally said, "You have guess-
ed well. I am in trouble and in the way you
say, but I am not guilty of wilful murder, yet
I dread the consequences of being apprehended.
At Fort Scott, Mo., I traded horses with a
jockey, and the next day he came to me and
said I should trade back, as I had cheated him
by lying about my horse. I told him that I
never traded back; when I traded and found
myself cheated I had to stand to my bargain,
and if I happened to make a good trade I
mean to keep it. He then grew furious and
said he would make me trade back, but I told
him he would do nothing of the kind, when
he flew at me with his raw-hide whip and
began whipping me over the head and face
with it. This was more than I could stand,
and, as he was a large bully, I drew my knife
and used it with fatal effect. I fled immediately, not because I was afraid of being
hanged, but I knew it would cause me a great
deal of trouble and cost me a large amount of
money to vindicate myself, as I had no friends

with me at the time, and I knew the few spectators to be very reckless and predjudiced against me. I have sent for my family to meet me at Lakin, and they will be there to-morrow or the next day, and I have been thinking that the officers may follow them and trace me out in that way. Now, what I want to know of you is this: Do you blame me for using my knife on him, and will you do anything against me? "

"No," said I, "I do not blame you at all, if it is the way you say, and will be glad to help you if I can. So if you have anything you wish me to do, let me hear it."

"I have nothing for you to do at present," said he, "except that when we go in to the Station, you go in first and find out if there are any strangers in town, and if they are from Ft. Scott, or that vicinity. If there are, I want you to pry around and find out what their business is, and report to me; if you find my family already there you can tell them how it is, and let me know as soon as you can see how the land lays."

I told him I would do so and in the morning started in without him. When I got in I noticed a stranger, but paid no attention to him then, and began getting rid of my load of meat, but soon the stranger came up to the wagon and began looking at the meat, remarking that it was the first he had ever seen.

"It is;" said I in feigned astonishment. "Where did you come from?"

"From Missouri, near Ft. Scott," was his answer.

Then I knew he was a detective, hunting for Howard, but thought him very stupid to tell where he was from and give himself away so easily. He took quite an interest in me and followed me about questioning me at every opportunity. "Let's see, what is your name?" he asked. I told him my name. "Do you hunt for a living." I replied in the affirmative.

"Do you hunt by yourself?"

"Sometimes I do."

"Have you any one with you now."

"Yes, but I do not know where he is."

"When are you going out again?"

I told him I could not tell, as it depended

entirely upon circumstances ; I might go out
the next day, and I might not go again for a
week or more. "Well," said he, "if you go out
to-morrow I would like to go with you." I
told him I would see about it and left him.
When I went to the hotel I found Howard's
family there sure enough, but the stranger
watched me so closely that I could have no
conversation with the wo man. I was very
roughly dressed and my clothes were bloody,
and I suppose the woman at first took me for
a desperado, reeking with the blood of his vic-
tims. As soon, however, as she found out that
I was the "old hunter" that her husband was
with, she manifested a desire to speak to me,
but was watching the stranger as well as I and
would not speak to me in his presence, for she
had noticed him getting on and off the cars
every time that she did, and had pretty well
divined his purpose. The first chance I could
get I told her where her husband was, and she
begged me to help them to outwit the detective
and get away. I promised her that I would do
so, and about ten o'clock that night slipped out,
went to Howard and reported what I had

seen and heard. I told him to keep still until the next night and I would try to get him out and away. I talked about the Station the next day, and spent some time in the company of the stranger from Ft. Scott. and in his presence announced my intention of soon going on another hunt, and told him that if my partner did not come back I would be pleased to have him go with me. He was anxious to do so and we parted fast friends, but when he got up the next morning, the woman and children that he had followed from Ft. Scott were gone. As soon as everything was still that night I harnessed up the team, and, taking Howard's family with me, drove to where he was concealed, and started them toward Colorado. telling them to keep hidden during the day and travel during the night, and they were soon out of the reach of the detective. I got back to the hotel in time to get up for breakfast with the rest, but when the detective missed Howard's family he looked sharply at me, as if he thought that if I chose I could tell how they got away. As good luck would have it, some one told him that a woman and children got on a train that passed during the night, and he boarded the first train and left on a false track. This is the last I ever saw of either of the parties, but have since heard that Howard was caught, taken back to Ft. Scott, tried and acquitted.

# CHAPTER XVII.

## HUNTING ON THE "RANGE," ETC.

THE events detailed in the preceding chapter resulted in leaving me without a hand, but I soon struck a man by the name of Henderson. He had a good team, and we were soon on our way to the "range" with two teams. We first went to White Woman Creek, and on the way saw hundreds of antelopes, but we were looking for buffalo, and did not disturb them. Not finding any buffalo we crossed the creek, where we camped for the night. I killed an antelope for supper, and the next day we moved on to Beaver Creek, and again stopped for the night, camping under the bluff about twenty yards from the water. It was cool, cloudy weather, and there was but little water in the creek, but when we got up in the morning we were surprised to find ourselves surrounded by water, the more especially so, because it had not rained at all during the night. We could not understand it, as the water had raised from four inches to six feet, and evidently did not come from any freshet above as the water was not at all muddy. We managed to get out by wading and getting uncomfortable wet. When breakfast was over we proceeded down the creek to investigate as to the sudden rise. I krew that the cause was some stoppage below, but could not tell, though very anxious to find out what it was. We had not gone far when we came to a big beaver dam which the beavers were hard at work repairing. Then the cause of the sudden rise in the creek flashed upon me. The dam had lately broken and let the water in the creek run out, and the beavers had filled up the break the day that we camped at night and the mystery of the night was explained.

As a little sketch of the habits of this singularly intelligent animal may prove of interest to some of my readers, I will stop long enough to give in brief words what I know of the beaver:

This animal is about three times as large as

(21)

the common coon, with which all are familiar. and always about the water. They are particularly adapted to the water, having webbed feet, and the power to stay under the water for a long time. They have a broad, flat tail which they use as a trowel, and strong, heavy teeth with which they cut down large trees. They build houses of sticks and mud in the shape of a circular arch, with the entrance under the water, and have the different lodges connected by pass ways. In order that they may always have water to play in, they frequently build large dams across the stream. These dams are built of mud, sticks, logs and even large trees, the latter they cut down with their teeth at some point in the creek above the dam, and carried to the proper place by floating it down the current. To one who never before saw a beaver town and dam, the sight is as much of a wonder to him as anything you could show him. But as space is limited I will give the beaver a rest and pass on.

Leaving the beaver dam that had caused us

so much astonishment, we passed down the creek about twenty miles and then went across to the Cold Train Lakes, where we found numerous antelope watering. I told Henderson that we would stop right there and kill a load of antelope. Henderson turned out the horses and I went to work and before night I had killed twenty-four. The next morning a large buffalo came in to water and I got him. This made our load and we pulled in to Sherlock, where we sold out for $71.00, one-third of which went to Henderson. We only staid in Sherlock over night and started out again, this time going on the bed of the Pawnee River, as I supposed the buffalo were there. But when we arrived we found that the Indians had been there and had chased them out of the country on horeback. It frightens them badly to chase them on horseback, and when thus started do not soon stop. Finding that we could get no buffalo there, I set in and killed a load of antelope, and we took them into Pierceville, the nearest station. We then took another shoot, going in south of

the Arkansas River. I had killed plenty of
buffalo there and supposed I could easily do so
again. We had only gotten about twenty
miles south when we came to where the
prairie had been recently burned.
We traveled two more days that we
did not see anything at all but the
burned prairie. The worst of all was, that
we had taken but very little grub along
with us, of course, expecting to find plenty of
game, but in this we were disappointed, as all
the game had been chased out by the fire. I
had two dogs along and they soon began to
manifest decided symtoms of hunger, but as we
had but a very little for ourselves we did not
think it exactly prudent to divide with them.
At last I saw a badger lying near his hole
and shot him for my dogs, but they would not
taste it at all. I thought perhaps they might
get hungry enough to eat it before they got
anything else, so I threw it into the wagon and
took it along. When we camped that night
I again offered them some badger, but they
were not ready for it yet. I dressed it and

roasted it nicely but they wouldn't have it
yet. I still left it before them and by morning they had it nearly devoured. The next
day, about 2 o'clock, we arrived on the north
fork of Cimarron Creek. About the time we
struck the creek, Henderson pointed to a hill
to the left of us and said, "There are four
buffalo heads; some hunter has been here
not long ago."

I jumped upon the wagon to see them,
but as soon as I looked I told him to squat
down for those heads were fast to the buffalo
yet. I took my gun, and, getting as close to
them as I dared, saw that one of them was a
cow and the other three were young ones. I
concluded to kill the cow first, and then I
would be pretty apt to get the whole lot. In
this I was right, for the old one never got up
after I shot her, and in two minutes I had
them all. It is useless to state that we had a
feast that night, dogs and all.

The next day we drove about ten miles,

when we got out of the burnt district, and I
got on a high hill, and, scanning the plains
with my field glass, I discovered a large herd
of buffalo about six miles ahead of us. We
drove as close as we could with the wagon,
and then I got out, and, shooting one down,
"got a stand" on them and killed all we could
haul in both wagons. As we were going in
we saw a large herd close to the road, and,
as we wished to pay them a visit when we
could take care of some of them, we waited
for them to move, not wishing to frighten
them. As soon as the buffalo moved out of
our way we drove past, and, when we reached
the station, disposed of our meat as fast as
possible, and, hiring a hand to go with us,
started back for the herd we had left. We
expected to find them on Bear Creek, as they
were heading that way, and, with that expec-
tation, we drove up the creek, looking for
them. After traveling about forty miles we
had a snow storm, which left us with about
six inches of snow, and we were compelled to
lay over for two days in the bed of Bear Creek.

On the morning of the third day as I was making a fire I heard a fearful racket near, and ran up the bank to see what it could be. When I got up the bank I saw a buffalo and four wolves fighting. The buffalo somehow got hurt in the loins during the fight and could no longer run. As soon as the wolves saw me they run off, leaving me in possession of the prize.

Despairing of finding the buffalo as I had expected, we turned south toward the north fork of Cimarron Creek, and found a herd of fourteen and got eleven of them. This made out our load and we again drove in.

When we got in to the station (Lakin) there were three men from New York who had never seen a live buffalo. They examined my load very closely, and finally asked me what I would charge to take them with me the next time I went out. They merely wanted to go along to see what they could see. I told them that I would let them go for a dollar apiece per day, and the bargain was soon closed.

As soon as we could get ready we started from Lakin and went south of the Arkansas River to the head waters of North Fork Creek, about thirty miles back. We camped for the night on the creek, and during the night a snow fell about four inches deep. We lay still until about 10 o'clock, when the snow began to melt, and we harnessed up and drove about fifteen miles up the creek, when I thought it was about time to strike some buffalo, and getting on a hill, where I could get a good view for miles, I took my field glass and "viewed the landscape o'er." I saw an immense number of horses and cattle in different directions, and, after looking some time, I espied a herd of buffalo, about five miles off.

When I went to the wagon and told my companions that I had found a herd of buffalo, they were very much elated, and we drove on toward the herd. We soon got on lower ground, and were out of sight of them for some time, but kept our course, and when we finally came in sight of them they were not

not more than a half mile off. We were then
as close as we dared drive. I usually crawl
on my hands and knees in the grass and get
as close to a herd as I wish, but this time the
ground was so cold and muddy that I did not
feel like crawling, but just ran toward them
until they began to get alarmed, and then
began shooting. I had to fire at long range
and after several shots I finally broke the
shoulder of one, and he soon dropped out of the
herd, not being able to keep up. I waited
until the wagon came up and put the dogs on
the crippled one and let them kill him, and
we would camp here for the night. The crippled buffalo made his way the best he could
after the herd, with the dogs laying him, until
he got on a rise in the ground, when the rest
of the herd, seeing the fight. turned and came
dashing back, and began to try to kill the dogs.
who, though laying at them all the time, kept
out of their way. They kept moving toward
us while they were fighting, and my New
York chaps began to get frightened and were
afraid they would come toward us, but I told
(22)

them there was no danger, and if they would come to me I would show them how to kill buffalo, but I could not get them any closer. Finding it useless to waste time with them. I went to within a hundred and fifty yards of the buffalo and began firing. The herd was paying no attention to anything but the dogs, and at every shot I fired a buffalo dropped. I kept up firing until there was but one left. and he seemed to suddenly·become conscious that he was alone and began to look for company, and started right toward the New Yorkers. They thought sure that they were gone and began darting here and there, but when the buffalo was fifty yards of them it stopped to see what they were, and I sent a bullet through its heart, and it dropped dead. The New Yorkers were greatly relieved when they saw their enemy fall, and I suppose that they believe to this day that I saved their lives, though they were in no trouble at all. I had then thirteen buffalo, with the sun only about an hour high and all of them to dress before I went to bed. My companions offered to help me and did the best they could, but even that was not much, as they were banker's and lawyer's clerks and had never seen a buffalo before. With the exception of three the buffalo lay in a radius of thirty feet, and I built a fire near the center and by about 12 o'clock we had them in the wagons.

We talked the remainder of the night, and the next morning we saw a herd of about three hundred near us. I pitched into this herd and got eight. This made all we could haul, and we started in to Lakin. When we arrived at the hotel the landlord asked me why I did not bring some antelope. I told him that I was out after buffalo and didn't look for antelope. He then asked if I couldn't go out the next day and get him some, and I replied that I would try.

I took my old Indian pony and started, and found a nice herd not far from the station, and, slipping up as close as I could, I killed three. I had with me a rope about twenty feet long that I used to picket my horse, and tied my horse to the neck of one of the antelopes, which was not dead yet, though I supposed that it was just about breathing its last. and went on after the antelope. I started on their trail, overtook them and killed six, and when I got back to where I had left my horse, he was missing, as was also the antelope I hitched to him. I started out after them and found the antelope leading the horse by the picket rope. I soon dispatched it and started round gathering up what I had killed. I tied their heads together, two and two, and threw them across my horse until I got them all on, then I went in driving my horse before me. I must have presented an odd appearance as I entered the station in this manner, but, be this as it may, I gave them a good supply of antelope and got my pay for them, too.

## CHAPTER XVIII.

ALMOST STARVED—EATING PRAIRIE DOGS—
A GREEN HUNTER'S RELIC—HUNTING AN-
TELOPE, ETC.

I REMEMBER once I started out on a hunt
to a range where I had been finding plenty of
game, but when I got there I found that the
lakes had dried up and the game had gone
elsewhere for water, and I drove three days
without killing anything, and I soon began to
get hungry and was compelled to go two days
entirely without food. At last I struck a
dog town, and by that time I was so hungry
that I struck it for something to eat. I had
never eaten a prairie dog and had not regarded
them as at all choice as an article of food, but
I turned my horses out and shot one of the
little varmints, fried him nicely and ate
him. He tasted so nicely that I tried
another, and another, and still another until
I had eaten six. Ordinarily a man could

not eat more than one, but I was so hungry
and had nothing to eat with them that I easily
got away with six. I then hitched up and
drove about forty miles when I fell in with a
man named Edward Day, who had just killed
a buffalo and had the humps with him. I told
him that I was as hungry as a wolf and would
like to have something to eat, and we stopped.
built a fire and cooked a good mess.

After dinner I asked him where the game
had gone, and he replied tha' he had seen a
large herd only about five miles from where
we were. This revived my spirits considerably
and I immediately started for them and killed
six. I camped there that night and the
next morning three men came to my camp in
a wagon. They had been out to kill buffalo,
but had failed, and started back with heavy
hearts. After we had talked a while they said
they would give me five dollars if I would
show them how to kill a buffalo. I told them
I would do so, and we were soon after the
game. The buffalo were very thick then and
we were not long in finding plenty. But the

one who offered five dollars to teach him how
to kill them was so much afraid of them that
I could hardly get him near enough to do so;
but I got him as close as I could and showed
him which one to kill and he fired away but
missed clear. I saw that I had a hard task
and must get him closer, so I shot and crippled
one and put him after it. It moved off slowly
and he fired some twenty shots at it without
any visible effect, and I moved him up within
fifty yards of it, but by this this time he was
so nervous that he shook as if he had an ague
fit, and missed again. The buffalo, seeing us
about to overtake it, turned for fight, and I
had to shoot it down at last. I told him to
shoot it quick before it was dead, and he ran
ran up and put a ball in its ham, and turning
to me handed me the five dollars. He thanked
me very kindly, asked me to skin its head,
and said he was going to have it stuffed and
when he was an old man he would exhibit it
to his grandchildren as a relic of his exploits
as a great hunter.

We then camped there for the night, but as

we had to build the fire of buffalo chips, my friends were too extremely nice to touch them and I had to gather all the fuel myself. I often found men when they were on the plains for the first time that were too dainty of taste to eat anything cooked by a fire made of this kind of fuel; but they soon get over their squeamishness and come to their senses.

About the only man I ever saw that took kindly to buffalo chips at first dash was an old fried of mine, with whom some of my readers are acquainted—he sometimes rolls pills—who came out to Kansas to look at the country, and while out called to see me. We went out after antelope, and stopping at the head of a small branch we found a small hole of water, at which I could see that the antelope had been watering freely. I told my friend that we would stop and get some of them. We unhitched the horse and got the buggy down in a draw where it would be out of sight of the game, and we sat down to take a lunch. While we were eating an antelope stepped in sight within twenty paces of

us and I picked up my gun, which happened
to be within reach, and killed it. In a few
moments two more came to the spot where
the dead one was lying and I saved both of
them. I then told my friend to build a fire
and I would skin the antelope, and we would
have some fresh meat. He said he would do
so and asked me where he would find some
wood. I pointed at some "chips" and told
him there was plenty. Contrary to my expectations he jumped right into them and
began raking them up with his hands, and it
was but a few minutes until he had a chunk of
bread in one hand and a lump of meat in the
other.

## CHAPTER XIX.

A SHORT time after the occurrences detailed in the last chapter, myself and a friend went out on a hunt. We struck out south of the Arkansas River until we came to the North Fork, which was about thirty miles, then we traveled up this stream for nearly thirty miles, when we went south near the Point of Rock, on the South Fork of Cimarron River. Here we struck a large herd of buffalo, which my friend tackled while I remained with the team. The buffalo were down in a hollow and when he fired on them they dashed right toward me. I did not want to shoot as we had a very wild team and I did not care to be ran away with, but they came so close that I picked up my gun and blazed away. In my haste I forgot to withdraw the gunstick, which I had inserted with some oiled tow to prevent its rusting, and strung two on the gunstick. I creased them on the loins and brought them both down, but the horses were about to become unmanageable, and I had to stop my shooting and give them my whole attention. When my friend came up he was surprised to see that I had killed two as he had heard me shoot but once.

We soon got our load and started back, and after driving fifteen miles we camped by a big spring for the night. About 9 o'clock the wolves, attracted by the smell of fresh meat, began to howl around us. We had a dog with us that would fight them, though he had no business with a wolf, and they finally came so near that they and the dog kept up a continual racket all night. He would rush out at them and chase them a short distance, when they would turn and drive him back to where we were lying, then he would bay them until he got them started, when he would drive them back again. This proceeding was repeated every few minutes during the whole night, and, as you may well imagine we did

not sleep a wink. The wolves were nearly
starved and seemed determined to have something to eat. At one time during the night it
was really exciting and not at all pleasant.
At one time when they had chased the dog
right up to us, one of them attacked him and
they fought viciously over and upon us for
some time, but we pulled our buffalo robes
over us as soon as we could and did not get
injured at all, but we we were not at all comfortable until the fight was over, the dog finally driving the wolf off. In the morning we
got up feeling worse than when we lay down,
but got to sleep good the next night.

## CHAPTER XX.

In a few days after this I started on another hunt, taking with me an editor who wanted to see a herd of buffalo. On the second night we camped on Carter Draw on a large lake. We had not stopped long before we discovered that the antelope were coming in great numbers to the lake for water. The next morning they began to come in before sunrise, and I told the editor that if he would get breakfast I would go out and try to kill some of them, and after a run of about an hour I got ten. As soon as breakfast was over, I drove around and gathered up the game, and then started in to Sycamore Station, about thirty miles distant, on

the Atchinson and Santa Fe Railroad, where
shipped the antelope to Fisher, the hotel
proprietor at Lakin.

From Syracuse we drove about forty miles
north, near White Woman Creek, where we
ran on to a large herd of buffalo, but as it was
about sundown when we discovered them we
only took a good look at them, and concluded
to wait unttl morning before we disturbed
them. It was a very large herd and closely
covered a half a mile square, and we went to
bed speculating on the big load we would get
in the morning, but when we got up not a
single buffalo was to be seen. The editor was
considerably discouraged, but it was easy to
follow the trail, and as soon as we could get
ready we started on after them, and, after
about fifteen miles travel, came upon them
lying down. I slipped on them as close as I
could and killed four. We dressed them and
again drove on, and when we were near what
is called the State Line Trail, I concluded to
finish my load with antelope, and began killing them. When I had killed seven we ran

across a fellow with a team, and I hired him
to take my load in to Sargeant Station and
ship it to Lakin, and I drove on. We traveled
east a few miles and stopped on a small lake
where the buffalo and antelope were watering.
During the night several antelope came near
us to get water, and the editor shot one or
them, his first, and, so far as I know, his only
antelope. About 10 o'clock the horse we had
picketed near us suddenly began to snort and
act very much frightened. I sprang to my
feet thinging that the Indians were on us, but
was surprised to see a large herd of buffalo
within fifty yards of us coming for water.
There were plenty of them within a few feet
us, and they surrounded the wagon and so
frightened one of our horses that he broke
loose. I could easily have killed several but
was afraid that it would frighten the horse
still more and make him leave us entirely,
and I could only stand and look at them. As
soon as they passed I went and got the horse
and we again lay down, but in a few minutes
a single buffalo came down for a drink and I

shot him. We then put on our clothes and dressed him and did not sleep any more that night. In the morning we drove about five miles, when we struck a large herd and got six of them. This finished our load, and by the time we had them dressed it was nearly night, but I proposed to my partner that as the moon would shine we might start in to the station.

Shortly after we started the sky became cloudy and the night grew dark and I lost my bearing, and for fear of getting still worse we stopped for day. When we went to picket our horses it was found that our tether had been left where we camped the night before, and were compelled to take it turn about holding the horses until daylight. We soon found where we were and pulled in to Aubery Station, sold what I could and drove on to Lakin. The editor published an accoant of our hunt in his paper, and if you ever see it you can compare it with this and see how they tally. On this hunt I killed seventy-two antelope and eleven buffalo, which, considering the circumstances, did pretty well.

When I arrived at Lakin I found two sportsmen from Connecticutt waiting for me. They wanted me to go merely as a pilot and they wanted to do all the shooting themselves. They had an armory of six guns: two breech-loading shot-guns, two breech-loading rifles and two 18-inch rifles. They were to give me three dollars a day as long as we were out, and as soon as I was rested we started south of the Arkansas River about twenty miles. Their forte seemed to be the shot-gun, and they wanted to go where there was plenty of fowls. It was new to me to see men want to get after ducks and snipes where they can find plenty of antelope and buffalo, but they wanted fowls and I found what they wanted. I took them to a large lake that was alive with ducks and kendricks. The kendrick is about the size of the guinea fowl, and its flesh is delicate and finely flavored. There was also a kind of snipe about the size of a quail. and its flesh is excellent. What with kendricks, snipe and the different kinds of ducks the lake seemed almost alive, and my sportsmen had a gay old time. They were particularly interested in the kendricks, and reg rded them as a great curiosity: they have long legs for wading and an extremely long bill, generally about seven inches in length. These men would not shoot at a bird except on the wing, and never fired on them when they were in a bunch, but would make them fly up and selecting one bring it down.

They kept up their sport until one of them in firing at a duck on the wing happened to shoot the other with bird shot, but as the shot they were using was small it did not kill nor seriously injure him, but it put an end to the hunt, and we went back to Lakin.

Here I found two more men waiting for me to pilot them out on a hunt. They were doctors from Chicago and we soon came to terms. We started the next morning and going about twenty came to a lake and stopped for the night. Here we found antelope and killed seven. The doctors had shot-guns and

kept blazing away at everything they saw.
The wolves seemed very hungry and came
howling around quite close to us and my doctors killed several during the night with their
stot-guns.

They were well pleased with the sport and
in the morning we harnessed up and started
to find some buffalo. But just at that time
nearly everybody was after buffalo and antelope, and some days one could see as many as
fifty wagons going in every direction for meat,
and would not know what to do if they should
happen to stumble on a herd. They were
around with anything they could get hold of,
including knives, pistols, shot guns, etc. They
would ask me if the buffalo would fight, and
some seemed to imagine that they could ride
right up by the side of one and kill it with a
pistol or knife, and if they found a herd they
would rush right up as if they expected them
to stand still until they caught them by the
tails and cut their throats. In fact their crazy
rush and racket frightened the buffalo and
antelope out of the country and caused them

to seek a refuge from the din and noise farther west, and they were so frightened that they did not come back for six months. Most of these fellows had been gulled into coming west by land agents to get cheap land and had been bitten. At any rate they had driven the buffalo off and we had to go back without any.

# CHAPTER XXI.

I WILL now call your attention to a buffalo hunt that I took with a man by the name of Edward Riley. We started out from Wallace Station on the K. R. Railroad. On the second day we found a very large herd. They were coming toward us, and as the prairie was on fire behind them they were in a general stampede. I left Riley with the team and killed five in a very few moments, but was not long before the fire was right on us and Riley became so much frightened that I could not hardly do anything with him, and while my attention was directed to something else he turned and drove off in a gallop to make his escape, leaving me alone to do the best I could. After going a

short distance he turned to come back, but by
this time the smoke was so dense that he
could not find me.  I went on and dressed the
buffalo that I had killed, but Riley did not put
in an appearance.  By this time the danger
from the fire was over and I waited
patiently until dark.  Still Riley did not
appear.  I began to cast about to see how I
was going to keep from freezing, as I had
left my coat on the wagon when I started
after the buffalo, and Riley had driven off
with it, leaving me in my shirt sleeves, and
the weather was very cold.  I finally took the
hindes of two of the buffalo that I had killed
and rolled myself up in them as close as I
could, and it was not long until they froze and
become as solid as a holler log.  Still I was
warm, but could not move at all.  I lay thus
until the sun was an hour high in the morning, and by dint of hard squeezing I managed
to crawl out of my prison and look around, but
no Riley was to be seen.

I went to the top of a high hill but could
not see him at all, though I could see for miles

in every direction. I did not see him until late in the evening when he came in sight. You can imagine how glad I was to see him when I tell you that I had not had a bite to eat since he had left me, over twenty-four hours before, as I had no matches to start a fire to cook it with. When he came up I got a bite to eat, and we loaded up our meat and started down Goose Creek. We had scarcely started when it began to spit snow and indicate a snow storm. We soon stopped and camped in a draw and in the morning we found that the snow had drifted around our tent to the depth of about four feet, though on the level it was only about six inches deep. We got out and started, but it was so cold and disagreeable that we had to stop again, and we soon found ourselves snow-bound. When it cleared off we began to make preparations to move out, but found our wagon so badly "snowed in" that it took us some time to shovel it out. After a hard tug we finally got into Wallace, just two weeks from the time we started.

When we drove in the people came running up to ask if we had seen or heard anything of the Indians. They then told that there had been a big fight in the vicinity of the station, in which twenty-eight Indians had been killed. They had given us up for gone, though we had never seen an Indian or thought of danger.

I will now tell you of a wild horse chase that I happened to get into a short time after my buffalo hunt. Three of us started out to take three herds, one apiece. We took four hands along with us. On the second day I killed a load of buffalo and and sent a man in to Lakin with it, and we went on until we found wild horses, then we camped and prepared for business.

I selected for mine a herd of twenty-six— twenty-five bays and a roan—while the other two took one a herd of twenty-two and the other a herd of twenty-four, and we started out to see who could do the best. The herds started in the same general direction, going northwest into Colorado about one hundred miles from where we started them. We passed through a dry country but finally struck a section where there had been plenty of rain and the grasswas good. Thehorses wanted to stay here and began circling about. After fifteen days' hard driving we drove into Lakin with fifty-six head.

I had a corrall prepared for the purpose, which was made of railroad ties set about eighteen inches in the ground with wings formed the same way leading into it. We got them in the corrall after some difficulty, but yet had a hard job on hand. They all had to be broken or handled. To do this an experienced cow-boy throws a lasso over the head of one and chokes him down, when he is bitted and held by long ropes until he gives up and consents to be led about. It is important that they be handled as soon as they are driven in before they have time to rest up. They should also be handled every day until they become perfectly docile.

In 1881 I started out from Aubrey on a buffalo hunt, and went north of the Arkansas

(25)

River. When I had gone about forty miles
I came to a small lake where I found signs
that buffalo had been there very recently. I
ascertained which direction they went and
started after them. When I had gone about
five miles I discovered a herd. I had two
teams and two men with me. I left the men
with the wagons and slipped up as close as I
could and wounded but one when they dashed
over a hill and out of sight, but I noticed that
they were bearing around the hill and ran
across to intercept them if I could do so. As
was running along I heard something behind
me, and, on looking around. saw a buffalo calf
which had evidently been asleep when the rest
dashed off and when it awakened it took right
after me. It was a small one and came right
to me. I seized it and held it until my men
came up with the wagons when we tied it and
put it in a wagon. When I got to the other
side of the hill I saw that the wounded one
had dropped close by the road side, but when
I got up to it I saw that one of its hams was
entirely gone. I was very much surprised,

but on looking up the road I saw a wagon with three men in it driving rapidly off. Lying the ground near the buffalo was a fine field glass, which the fellows who stole my buffalo ham had dropped in their haste. After I had examined it I considered myself well paid for my ham and appropriated it. We camped only about a mile off, and when we got up in the morning saw two of the fellows riding back and forth looking, as I naturally supposed, for a field glass, but I doubt if they found it. We drove a few miles that morning and found five buffalo but only got one, when it began to rain and we had to go into camp. We laid up till the rain was over and started in. My calf died on the journey, but I killed enough antelope to make out a good load.

For the information of any person East who may chance to read this little book, I will devote part of this chapter to a brief description of Western Kansas generally, and the rivers and river valleys in particular.

Beginning at the northwester corner of the State and coming south the first river is the

Republican River, which heads in Colorado near, the foot of the mountains, and when it comes into Kansas is about sixty yards wide and is fed by springs. The Republican River has several southern tributaries, many of which are supplied with water and skirted with some timber, though not enough to make it a good location for saw mills. The next stream of note as you go south is Solomon River, which in the extreme western part of the State is a small stream and has no water, but lower down it receives the waters of many large springs and becomes quite a stream. This stream is skirted in places with some small timber and there are some good locations for ranches in this valley. South of Solomon River is Cold Goose Creek, which is fed by springs, and has some timber. There is good mowing in many places and it has a fine valley for ranches. The next stream south is South Smoky River. This has plenty of water and some timber. It is a good stream for ranches, but is nearly all taken up.

South of the Arkansas River are many

streams, some have plenty of water and others have not. There are many fine places for ranches on them.

All this is in the valley of the Arkansas River, and with its streams of water and good grazing is the best buffalo region on the globe.

My buffalo hunting has not been confined at all to Kansas, but I have frequently gon into Nebraska, Colorado, New Mexico, Indian Territory and Texas, in fact, there is hardly a square mile of western Kansas and the contiguous territory that I have not explored. I think perhaps that I am better acquainted with it than any other living man. There is not a creek that I cannot describe, not a skirt of timber that I have not seen or a range of hills that I not familiar with.

## CHAPTER XXII.

### CONCLUSION.

AND now dear reader as the space allotted to this little book is taken I will say a few words by way of conclusion and bid you adieu. I wish only to say in conclusion that in this little book is no attempt at fanciful destriptions of imaginary adventures or flowery style of narration, but it has been my aim to state only facts and these in the briefest manner practicable, and if you do not consider it sufficiently romantic and exciting please remember that it is not a dime novel, but, so far as it goes, a true history of my life on the plains. Please remember, also, that it was hurriedly written while on a visit to my old home and my aged father in Warrick Co., Indiana, after an absence of sixteen years, and that but few of my adventures are related, though enough, I hope, to give you an idea of the wild life I have led on the plains.

Should any of my old acquaintances in old Hoosierdom ever visit Western Kansas, they will find me on a ranch near Granada, Colorado, where I will be glad to entertain them, show them the country, or, if they wish, take them out on a buffalo hunt.

But as the time allotted to this visit has drawn to a close, and as I must return to my ranch and my family, this volume must close.

THE END.